THE TILTING ROOM

The Tilting Room

stories
by
RON BUTLIN

CANONGATE
1983

First published in 1983
by Canongate Publishing Ltd
17 Jeffrey Street, Edinburgh

© Ron Butlin
1983

ISBN 0 96241 050 9 Hardback
ISBN 0 86241 051 7 Paperback

The publishers acknowledge
the financial assistance of
the Scottish Arts Council
in the publication of this
volume.

Typeset by Witwell Ltd Liverpool
Printed by Redwood Burn Ltd
Trowbridge

ACKNOWLEDGEMENTS

I would like to thank the Scottish Arts Council, the University of Edinburgh and Deans Community High School who have allowed me time to complete this book.

Some of these stories have been published in the following magazines: AMF, Bananas, Cencrastus, Scottish Short Stories (Collins 1981, 82, 83), New Edinburgh Review, Firebird 1 (Penguin 1982), Words, Radio 3.

For Jim, who would always listen
and for Robert who would never stop talking

CONTENTS

1

2

3

1

Journal of a Dead Man

I am called Samuel, but I am not a Jew. Would the Germans believe that? I am afraid of the Germans, they do terrible things my father told me about.

I am lying in bed when they come. They shine a torch into my eyes and say: Jew, come with us. It is alright because I am not Jewish I say to them. I know that you have your orders but it is all a mistake. However, they make me get dressed and I give them cigarettes because they seem to be nice boys really, not yet twenty, and they don't know what it's all about.

Outside there is a lorry with 'Juden' written on the side. The back of it is a cage, and there are Jews in it. It is not your fault, I say to the guards who sit with sten-guns across their knees and look at me with their steady blue eyes. I am not Jewish, I say with a laugh, but that's not your fault, you are not to know that. It will all be sorted out with your superiors when we arrive, I tell them. We are driven to an enormous building – that is, it feels enormous, I can't see it of course, because of the dark.

I climb out of the lorry and am taken down stairs at the side of the building. From there we go by lift through basements and sub-basements down many levels. The guards do not mistreat me as I expected they might, but when I stumble once or twice, then they hit me across the shoulders with the butts of their rifles; but it is not their fault, they think I am Jewish. Soon it will be sorted out and their chief will be giving me a drink upstairs in his office. He will apologise for the unfortunate error and inconvenience, saying that these things happen.

Then, as I expected, I am indeed called up to the Director's office and he apologises to me profusely. He shakes my hand cordially as we bid each other good-bye, and asks me if I would like to see how the Jews are looked after. I reply that it's alright, I know that the work has to be done and I am certain that they do it well. Then his gentle German eyes gaze into mine, and he says that now I am here I must take the opportunity to see how it is done; then more firmly he says that it is really my duty to see that such work is carried out properly. He smiles; we go downstairs, he and I, in the company of two guards. On the way, he gives a descriptive tour of the building, and finally we arrive outside the room where he says 'they' are kept.

When we walk in all the Jews flatten themselves against the walls and beg forgiveness. I whisper to one of them that I would like to forgive them and I don't want to hurt them really, but I am just there to watch by invitation of the Director. By forced invitation, I add with emphasis. The guards then bring some of them into a room like a hospital theatre and stick electrodes onto parts of their bodies. Then one of them switches on the current. I cannot look away because the Director is looking at me.

After two Jews have been dealt with like that, the switch is put into my hand and I am the one who must control the current. I know that it is not my fault because I am being forced to do it. Just before I turn on the current-switch, the Jew who is on the table asks me my name, I do not want to say Samuel so I say Sam. Then he says, can't I hear the Lord calling me? I say nothing. The Director suggests that I make that Jew hear the word of the Lord, so I give him a blast of current and he writhes. Did you hear that ? I say to him.

The Director comes up to me and says softly, it is a job that has to be done and you have proved yourself. He kisses me on both cheeks and there are tears of joy in his eyes.

Yesterday, while I was working in the supermarket, my wife came across some photographs of Ruth. They had been taken at her flat one evening during dinner; as each course was served she had removed some of her clothing. My wife ripped up all the pictures. She told me that I was too old for that sort of thing, but I know that I am not too old to fall in love.

I do not love my wife. I do not even think of her very much; but I think of Ruth a lot, though I know she cannot marry me.

Sometimes in the evening when we are watching television, I look at my wife and think, 'You middle-aged bitch, you are fat and ugly and stupid, and I have nothing to say to you anymore, and you have nothing to say to me.'

Then I think about Ruth. When I get into bed and make love to my wife, I try to remember all I can about Ruth until, for a few seconds, it is as if my wife becomes Ruth. But afterwards I am sad because I know that it was only my imagination.

Ruth is growing younger and more beautiful each year. She is becoming more intimate with me. Every time I recognise her I cut out her picture: I have many photographs of her now. Sometimes when my wife is out, I will close the curtains and switch on the small table-lamp, and then I will spread some of her pictures on the floor and gaze at them. Though she seems to be a different woman in each one, I recognise her for she is the woman I love when she leans back on a couch to pull on her stockings, and when she is sunbathing beside a deserted swimming-pool.

This evening I was looking at a photograph of her stepping out of a long white dress. She knows that her breasts are glorious because I have often told her so, and she touched them then while her eyes met mine. I looked very closely until once again I felt the caress of her fingertips and her tongue, and breathed in her scent, and felt the silk and lace against my skin. I gazed at her photograph until I knew she was there and heard her calling my name. Then I looked across the room to where she was stepping out of her long silk dress as once more she came towards me out of the darkness.

Every time I am taken into the basement by the Germans, I am not really very afraid because I know that it will always work out in the end. I know that although I will be forced to work the machine, the Germans will be my friends afterwards. But each time it happens they take longer and longer to believe that I am not a Jew, and in order to prove it I must do more and more work with the machine 'to make them hear the word of God' as the Director says.

I cannot tell one Jew from another, so really I am dealing with the same Jew each time. And the Germans really all look the same except for the Director who wears a suit whereas the rest of them are in uniform. One night, however, a Jewess is brought in, and she is beautiful. The Director asks me if I want to have her before she goes on the machine. He says that at this moment she will be at her best, adding that she will do anything in the hope of release. I guess that this is one last trick of his to make me betray my suspected jewishness and so I say yes, thinking that I will show him once and for all. Well, he says, she's all yours now.

She is standing rigid with fear and then, as I approach her, she spits at me. I get two of the Germans to take an arm each and hold her against the wall. She starts swearing at me and calling me a pig, and asking how could I, a Jew like herself, be here with these Germans and do this to her? I tell her that I am no Jew but she calls me a liar. I am standing only a few inches from her now and she turns her face this way and that, screaming that I am a Jew – and so to shut her up I grab her by the hair and kiss her on the mouth.

She tries to bite me but I am too quick for her and step back a pace. She is wearing a kind of hospital gown which is very unbecoming. Taking it in both hands I rip it open, and now I can see how beautiful she is! Behind me, the Germans are shouting encouragement, giving cat-calls, whistling and clapping their hands. One of the guards holding her says in a low voice that it will go much easier for her if she doesn't struggle so much, she's going to get it anyway so she might as well relax and enjoy it. The other one, however, says that as she's going to get it anyway she may as well struggle if she wants.

As she raises her eyes to meet mine I see for the first time that it is Ruth. The shouting and the hand-clapping seem to be coming from further and further in the distance. She looks at me and says nothing. She and I are standing in total silence and then, out of the corner of my eye, I notice that though the guards still seem to hold her, this is an illusion; for I see that really it is as if the soldiers are painted onto the wall, and only by some sleight or trick of line do they appear to hold Ruth there.

Effortlessly then, Ruth places her hands on my shoulders and turns me round. Immediately I see that the Director and the guards are also painted; they are cut-outs that are aging visibly and turning yellow even as I stand here. The basement is becoming very dirty and the walls are silently cracking apart. Ruth kisses me. The ceiling is disintegrating and I watch as unfamiliar stars drift slowly across the night sky.

My hand that is caressing her breast is trembling and becoming wrinkled. My breath is becoming more and more strained with effort. I must make love to her, she says. Her voice and caresses encourage me urgently. Above me now the stars are whirling dizzily. The walls have disappeared. Every kiss and every caress is an effort for me. She is holding me so tight and I am becoming frailer and frailer. I must make love to her she says, and I am certain that I am dying.

Then I see in her eyes that I must die and that she has known this from the very beginning. I know now that I must make love to her and in the certainty of this I begin to climax and to die. Even as I do so the stars begin to slow down, I am an old man recognising for the first time Ruth's love for me shining in her eyes as darkness comes over me, and bliss.

I had a dream last night: I was working in the store as usual and every woman there was Ruth. She was sitting on the counter and she was leaning against the shelves, and each one was gazing lovingly at me. Then she turned round from the end of one of the aisles and began walking towards me. As she approached she began undoing her blouse. Behind her I saw the manager come out of his office, it was the Director and he smiled at me. I heard laughter outside – the German guards were crowded at the shop window pressing their faces against the glass. But Ruth seemed unaware of all these people, she kept walking towards me and discarding her clothes. I tried to warn her but I couldn't speak. I was unable to move.

When she saw that I did not respond to her, she looked very hurt. Then she began to let her hands run gently over her body, they caressed her breasts and stroked between her thighs; and all the while the guards cheered loudly. I watched in horror and could do nothing. She became more and more excited; the cheering of the guards outside grew louder and louder as more of them pressed against the glass. Her breathing quickened. The Director was standing beside me and he gave me a conspiratorial wink. All at once I was able to speak – and just as I shouted to her, the glass in the window gave way and the store was filled with Germans.

Always she comes to me out of the darkness, and afterwards she returns there. I switch off the table-lamp, open the curtains and finally I put away the pictures without looking at them again. My hand is shaking and often I feel very sad because I love her. I love her so much and I am with her for only so few moments at a time. For the rest it is days and years spent alone, time I cannot share with her.

My wife does not know what love is, or she has forgotten. Even when I am in the basement with the Germans and being made to work the machine, I have not forgotten Ruth – for at that moment I long for her so much that afterwards the guards sometimes have to unclasp my hand, finger by finger from the switch.

This morning I rose from the dead. It is a time to perform miracles. My wife had betrayed me to the Germans saying that I was a Jew and a degenerate, and I looked at dirty pictures.

They came for me last night, took me in the lorry and down into the basement. They tied me to the table and turned on the machine.

But now I have risen from the dead. My wife is lying on the couch watching television. She has destroyed all the pictures of Ruth so as to keep us apart.

Ruth is not dead, she cannot die because she is younger and more beautiful each time she comes to me. But she is trapped in the darkness and I am trapped here.

My wife has forced us apart, but now she must bring us together. It is a time for miracles. She must dress as Ruth dresses that her body will grow younger and more beautiful.

My wife is dying and Ruth is coming towards her out of the darkness. Her body will be draped in silk and lace, and Ruth will gaze lovingly at me through her eyes.

We will be together for all time, because we who have risen from the dead become younger each day and never die.

The Germans are dead, my wife is dead; everyone is dead who has not been on the machine.

There are wounds on our hands and feet made by the machine, and it is by these that we recognise those whom we love and who will live forever.

Scenes from an Opera

There is a flight of stairs leading up to the next floor. I live under these stairs. I crouch to cook and lie full-length to sleep. I have been living here for two years. I bother nobody and nobody bothers me – some of the friendlier residents even bid me good-day as they pass. One morning I found a mop and pail beside me when I woke-up. 'A strange gift,' I thought to myself – the pail and mop being completely new – then I realised what was expected of me in return for my lodgings: that day and twice a week from then on, I cleaned the stairs.

Occasionally people left food out for me, but not now. The main door was locked three days ago and a list of the residents' names was pasted up on each floor. I am on the list as 'Cleaner – third floor.' Already some of the names are stroked out. No-one can enter or leave the building. There is a notice which says that anyone seen climbing out of the windows will be shot on sight.

Usually I spend the afternoons seated on the window-sill at the end of the corridor, looking down into the street. But nothing happens or else it happens too quickly: a window smashes, a building collapses or someone is killed. There is the occasional explosion or burst of gunfire but it is always over too soon to see exactly what is happening. I have not had a cigarette since yesterday and there is a rumour that the drinking water is poisoned.

It is late afternoon. I am looking out of the window and swaying slightly as I sing to myself 'Im Mohrenland gefangen war' from Mozart's 'Seraglio'. I understudied the part of Pedrillo when I was training to be a singer – four completely wasted years as it turned out. I climb off the window-sill, then walk over to one of the flats and ring the bell.

Nothing happens and so I knock. The door seems to be made of heavy wood. It appears solid and is painted a very bright green. It is being opened slowly. I stand up straight when a woman appears who could be Blondin out of 'The Seraglio'.

'Yes?' she begins. Then she recognises me. 'Oh! it's you.'

'Who is it?' a voice asks from backstage. Blondin steps back into the flat.

'The cleaner,' she replies waiting for me to develop the situation. By gesturing I try to tell her that I am hungry and also I would appreciate a cigarette.

'What does he want?' the voice comes again. A deep voice. Osmin's.

'Just a minute,' she says and closes the door. I stand and wait. There is a burst of machine-gun fire offstage, and people shouting. But I don't go to the window; I wait.

Several moments pass and I am still standing outside the flat. It is almost dark now, the lights on the stairs have not been working for the last few days. Someone is coming along the corridor. I will walk beside him trying to tell him that I am hungry.

'Aren't we all?' the man remarks and he goes into a flat further down the corridor. I walk a few steps then sit on the floor, my back against the wall.

A moment later the man comes out of his flat, calls to me, then throws me a couple of cigarettes. He doesn't wait to be thanked but goes back inside again. Offstage right there is a loud explosion. The entire floor shakes. I go over to the window to smoke one of the cigarettes while looking down into the street. When it is finished I feel my way to my bed under the stairs where I lie in the darkness staring at nothing until I fall asleep.

It is morning. I am drinking some of the water that is rumoured to be poisoned. I was awakened during the night by someone hammering on the street-door to get in, then the hammering stopped and I went back to sleep. When I got up I tried a few doors but no-one answered. Some more of the names on the list are stroked out – they will have died. Perhaps it is not

the water as there seem to be quite a few old people living here.
Once all the names in a flat are stroked out, then it will be empty
and I can break in to secure it for myself.

I will knock on the door of the man who gave me the cigarette
in the last scene.

He invites me in. This is the first time I have been inside one of
the flats. The man tells me that he shares it with his wife and her
mother; they have no children. His mother-in-law is very fat and
appears to be completely deaf. He says that she never moves
from her chair and it seems she'll never die. He adds that
unfortunately his wife loves her, otherwise he'd have dealt with
her years ago.

In this scene there is clothing hanging everywhere. There is a
radio on the sideboard. It is tuned into a foreign station – so
perhaps the mother-in-law is not deaf, but simply does not
understand English. Three tables are set round her heaped with
objects to fill up her day. On television, with the sound down, is a
programme about underwater life. The atmosphere is stifling.
When she speaks to me I don't understand a word she says. Her
voice is a pleasant contralto. Then she turns slightly and spits
into a small basin on one of the tables beside her. She begins
rummaging about in the articles on the table – magazines, pens,
cigarettes, a whistle, some sewing – and she beckons me to come
closer. There is quite a growth of hair on her chin and upper lip.
She smells very unpleasant especially when her movements
disturb her clothing. Possibly she isn't so much fat as very
swollen and in great pain all the time.

At last she has found what she has been looking for – a piece of
cake which she offers me. Her son-in-law tries to interfere but she
glares at him and he does nothing. As I eat it her face relaxes into
a smile. However I sense that she will now want to pat or fondle
me perhaps, and gradually I move out of reach. The cake has
made me thirsty. I am trying to ask them for something to drink
when the room is shaken. There is an explosion; the windows
rattle and one of the panes cracks right across.

A woman's voice, an alto, comes from a room to the left. She is
calling for the man, Robert, who goes leaving the fat woman and

myself together. She smiles broadly then points firstly to the window and then to the room into which Robert has gone. She is talking very excitedly – I don't understand a word of it, of course. Suddenly she breaks off to spit into the basin again. When I go over to a sink in the corner of the room for a cup of water the woman shouts at me – she is probably warning me about the poisoned water; her daughter must have told her. I pay no attention.

Robert returns from the room and asks me my name. I try to say it. Sometimes I can almost manage something, but not today.

He gives me a pencil and paper. I write very casually though my hand trembles. First name? Robert demands – and I begin to write again but the pencil breaks. For some reason Robert has taken offence at such clumsiness and, completely ignoring my renewed attempts to sound out my name, states curtly that *his* name is Sinclair. He adds that as his wife would like a word, I should follow him.

The bedroom is tastelessly furnished from budget catalogues. The curtains are drawn. Very harsh lighting comes from a coiled silvery object which stands on the bedside table. Robert's wife looks very weak.

'My husband...' she begins and then stops. 'He can *hear*, can't he?' she asks in an aside.

'I think so; yes, he can,' comes the reply after a moment's pause.

'My husband...' she starts once more then trails off again. She picks up a reel of cotton from the folds of the bedspread and begins snapping pieces of thread.

'I shall come straight to the point,' she declares firmly and sits up in bed. 'You are the cleaner and – what did you say your name is?' she asks, then without waiting for a reply she continues. 'Well then, Whatever-you-call-yourself,' her voice has suddenly become contemptuous in tone, 'why aren't you out fighting? Don't you care that they might break in here to rape and murder us all? Do you wish me and my mother dead?'

I shake my head and feel very embarrassed; she must be very ill to speak like this. I glance over to her husband with a look of understanding and pity. But Robert glares back at me.

She continues snapping the thread in silence for a moment. Then she begins again.

'My husband has to stay here to look after my mother and myself. But you – you've no family have you? No-one depends on you for anything do they? So don't act so selfishly!' She falls back against the pillows quite exhausted with her performance.

Robert goes to her side. He gives her something to drink and then sits on the bed holding her hand in his. He kisses her gently on the forehead then turns to face me.

'Don't just stand there. Aren't you ashamed of yourself?' he asks. His wife smiles then, by gripping tightly to her husband, raises herself up again.

'Why don't you do something for once, something amusing?' she sneers. 'Make us all feel good for a change. I'm in bed. I'm dying – amuse me!' She begins pointing at me and shouting, 'Come on you bastard, you creeping little bastard, amuse me!'

And when she sees me leaving at this point she starts screaming the crudest obscenities after me. Her husband joins in. I rush through the kitchen where the fat woman immediately enters in counterpoint to her daughter and son-in-law. Her timing is perfect and her contralto soothing. She blows me a kiss; I give her a wave as I make my exit.

The corridor looks chilly after the closeness of the flat. When I look at the list again I notice that some of the names have been crossed out in red, some in blue – so different people must mark off who's died. But if it is the people in the flats who mark off their own dead, it surely follows that there will never be a flat with everyone's name stroked off – for the last person can hardly be expected to cross off his own name.

There may be a flat empty at this moment! All I need do is look for the flats with only one name left and try them. Scanning the list eagerly I notice that there are two flats worth trying on this floor. The first is three doors along. I will try it.

I ring the bell. I ring it again. What if no-one answers? It is possible I will have to break down the door. Break the lock maybe. There was a time when I could have forced my way in with a piece of plastic – but nowadays the locks are better made, more's the pity. Or I could drive wedges into the top and bottom of the door – then the tensions will build up between the door, the frame and the lock until the weakest part gives way. Noisy, but no-one would pay the slightest attention.

I am about to ring the bell for one last time when a voice asks who's there. I mustn't move. The voice asks again, and again gets no reply. The door remains shut. The owner must be standing still and listening closely. I walk quietly round to the other flat. I ring the bell and wait.

There is no reply. I ring again and again there is no reply. I knock loudly and still there is no reply. It must be empty, so I will break in.

There are two locks on this door, large ones. I step back then slam my shoulder against the panel. I hurt my shoulder. Stepping back again I then kick it twice, hurting each foot in turn. Time to rest. Perhaps I should wait until someone else dies – someone with smaller locks. What I need is a tool of some sort – an axe or a crowbar. But as it seems unlikely I could borrow one, I sit down opposite instead, and stare at the door.

There is a small window set above the lintel to let light into the hallway. Not a big window certainly – but if I managed to smash it and climb in without bleeding to death, then I wouldn't need to bother with the door. What I need is a handy prop to break the glass – and there is a fire-extinguisher at the end of the hall. I will use that.

Fighting has begun again off-stage: machine-gun and mortar fire. Bullets hit the main door downstairs and echo loudly. Then someone begins hammering and shouting to be let in. There is another burst of gunfire against the door followed by a scream. I hurl the fire-extinguisher through the window, clamber onto the lintel, squeeze past the broken glass and then jump down onto the floor.

The flat is in darkness. I grope my way along the passage and into one of the rooms. The furniture is large and old, but looks quite comfortable. It is a bedroom – there are two bodies, a man on the bed and a woman on the floor. Very cautiously I open the window and push them out. As each one falls to the ground there is a burst of gunfire. I close the window before going to look round my flat.

After a meal of corn beef and pineapple slices I settle down to watch television having placed a bottle of sherry and a packet of cream crackers within reach. There is a schools' programme about transportation; a consumer phone-in; and then, to my delight, a filmed performance of Mozart's 'Seraglio'. I relax into my chair and dip a cracker into my cup of sherry.

During the rather laboured finale to Act 2 the door-bell rings. I ignore it. It rings again and again I ignore it. Suddenly there is a gunshot and the door is forced in. A chorus of soldiers enters shouting in a foreign language. I try to show them that I cannot speak. One of them, however, is very impatient and shoots at the TV screen. There is silence. Then he points the gun at me.

At this cue another soldier enters; the chorus stands to attention. He must be an officer.

'We are soldiers of the army of liberation. Until everything is over you must remain indoors.' He has a good voice, a tenor, with only the slightest trace of accent. Having glanced quickly round the kitchen he looks into the hall.

'You have room for four soldiers,' he states. I nod in agreement. Four soldiers are picked to remain and one of them, Rall, is placed in charge. The rest leave.

The five of us sit down to finish the sherry. An enormous slab of cooking-chocolate is produced and shared out. By way of introduction each of them points to himself and says his name. I write down the name 'Donaldson' – which is the name on the door. I can't help laughing at the sounds they make when trying to say this name. Soon the soldiers join in the laughing as well. Everyone shakes hands and another bottle of sherry is opened.

Suddenly there is a ring at the door-bell. I get up to answer it but Rall motions me back to my seat and answers it himself. He returns with Robert, the man who invited me into his flat. Robert is crying. He is given a lengthy solo in which he says that soldiers forced their way into his flat then raped his wife. When he tried to

stop them they threatened to shoot him. What could he do? His
mother-in-law was a collaborator, he says – and now she is dead.
To make things clearer he begins acting out the events he is
describing. He shows us some blood on his clothes, then he
brings out a knife. At this, Rall shoots him. He falls to the floor.
Two of the soldiers drag the body off-stage.

Evening, a few days later. I am asleep on the couch in front of
the stove. Rall enters with some food and wakes me. I have
started preparing the evening meal when he tells me he has a
surprise: when the other soldiers return, he announces, they will
be bringing a woman. Women have been brought back before,
but this time the woman will be for me.

And a few moments later the other soldiers enter with Robert's
wife. She seems very ill, perhaps even dying; she is still wearing
her nightdress. They put her in the bedroom then go through one
at a time until it is my turn.

She is lying on the bed and seems hardly aware that someone
else is in the room. I stand and look at her. After a few moments I
cross over to sit on the edge of the bed. Still she seems unaware of
what is happening. When I take and kiss her hand she looks at
me in disgust then turns her face away. She does not seem to
recognise me. I kiss her hand again. Then suddenly grabbing her
shoulders and twisting her round, I kiss her very roughly on the
lips. She doesn't struggle; she makes no response at all. When I
let go she falls back on the bed and lies still. Her nightdress is up
round her waist – I smooth it down gently. My hand rests on her
knee for a moment. I take it away and am about to stand up
when the soldiers rush into the room.

They begin shouting at me and pushing me against her. They
are joking and angry at the same time. They sing a robust comic
quartet – each taking a verse to tell and act out what he'd done
with her; the chorus is an unexpectedly gentle lyric in praise of
women and love. At the same time, they are forcibly undressing
me while one of them rips open the front of the woman's
nightdress.

Having stripped me naked they stand me on my feet, then

wait. Robert's wife has been made to sit up in bed; her face is expressionless. Rall points his gun at me making the other soldiers laugh. I don't move. Rall suddenly fires his gun past me, shattering one of the window-panes. I remain standing exactly where I am. But the woman gets up off the bed and comes towards me. She is terrified. As she takes me in her arms the soldiers give a loud cheer.

She presses herself against me; she says that the soldiers might kill us if nothing happens. She keeps shouting at me, asking if I understand. I give no response. Desperately she begins caressing me and saying things to get me excited. She says her name is Mary but she will be whoever I want. Finally she says we should pretend. Then lying down she pulls me on top of her and begins to moan gently.

A week later. I am standing at the sink washing dishes; Mary is looking out of the window. The kitchen is as before except there is a blackboard set up on the mantelpiece. On it are four columns of chalkmarks. The dishwater looks slightly greenish – it must be poisoned. Mary remarks that as the streets are full of tanks perhaps the rumours are true – and the soldiers really are going to leave in the next few days. I embrace her and we kiss.

She goes over to the blackboard. In an impassioned aria she calls them bastards because even when they've won they're still killing people. Even when they've won they're still playing it like a game and keeping scores. And tomorrow, with any luck, they'll go away; but what will be done with the blackboard – just wipe it clean? She is about to pick it up when I grab her and hold her still. Gradually she calms down. She agrees that would have been a stupid thing to do. Only a few days more, she says, maybe even tomorrow.

I begin looking at the blackboard. My arms are folded and I am staring very hard. All at once I smile and then laugh. Mary looks at me in amazement. I am really excited, waving my arms about. I will try to show her why.

First I turn her round to face the blackboard; then I go over to it and rub out two of the chalkmarks on two of the columns. I turn to her, looking very pleased with myself.

Mary doesn't understand. To explain to her what I think will happen now, I decide to do a charade. I will pretend to be each soldier in turn.

The first one comes in and chalks his day's score then adds it all up to himself. The second soldier does the same. But when the other two add up their scores they discover the totals are less than they should be. They check them again. Then they accuse the first two, who deny everything. None of them will suspect me – why should they? A fight starts and eventually they shoot each other.

Mary agrees that it will probably work, adding that just to be on the safe side perhaps we should go into her flat until it is all over. We leave.

After a few moments the soldiers enter and the finale begins.

The German Boy

The woman I can see standing outside in the pouring rain reminds me of Klaus, the German boy. It is the expression on her face: she looks so desolate, so utterly unloved. People hurry past her as quickly as possible; if someone does smile, I watch her hesitate for a moment. Then she looks away.

When I came to the office about half-an-hour ago I passed her by pretending interest in a shop-display. From here, however, I can study her in perfect safety. Perhaps she is waiting for someone. I realise now that she could not have been taken in by my elaborate charade for it is repeated every few minutes by others – repeated too frequently to be convincing. At one time I might have pitied her, for that kind of cruelty comes easiest of all. Believe me, I know – Klaus taught me that.

This morning I have come to the office and done nothing. There is a pile of correspondence for me, some of it marked 'urgent' – instead I stand and stare out of the window at the well-dressed woman opposite. She is in her mid-forties. I think she is crying but it is difficult to tell at this distance. She has glanced in my direction so I will move back from the window.

I remember my headmaster talking to us before Klaus was brought in. 'There is nothing special about him,' he said, 'remember, he is just like the rest of us.'

When he came into the classroom for the first time, however, it was quite obvious he was not like the rest of us: Klaus looked different, he talked different and, even though he wore the same clothes as us, somehow he seemed to be dressed differently. Everyone looked at him and he looked at the floor. He had fair hair, very pale skin, and was quite tall. His shoulders were trembling – an action his long arms increased proportionally, making his hands jerk as if they were receiving a series of small electric shocks.

'This is Klaus, he is going to join your class.' The headmaster was a small red-faced man who always looked as if he was too small and too red-faced to be comfortable. When he died a few months later from sunstroke I imagined him as having simply exploded one very hot afternoon.

My family talked a great deal about 'class' which for a long time I confused with my schoolfriends who were all of one class in both senses of the word. 'He is of a different class altogether' meant, to me, that someone was simply a few years older or younger than myself. And when my Aunt Claire happened to remark during an Open Day that Klaus was of a different class to the rest of the boys, I hastened to correct her saying that on the contrary he was the same age as myself and we sat next to each other and were the very best of friends. She said I was a very kind and thoughtful boy; and I replied excitedly that I was going to learn German. 'Of course you should help him to be at his ease, but you mustn't neglect your proper studies,' she concluded with a smile.

Klaus didn't even glance at the class he was about to join. He looked more uncomfortable than ever: his knees began shaking and his hands, in an effort to control the effects of the 'electric shocks', had grasped his jacket tightly at the sides – which served only to increase his nervous jerkings by the amount of 'give' in the material.

The headmaster ushered him to one side of a map of the world which had the British Empire coloured red, 'An unfortunate choice of colour,' my aunt had observed during her visit. Then he indicated Germany and spoke to Klaus in German: he replied 'Ja, mein Herr' without raising his eyes from the floor. And then a moment later he did look up – not at the map, however, but at us; and he smiled, then blushed and returned his gaze to the floor. A boy sniggered. The headmaster plodded on.

'Klaus is from Germany. This is Germany.' He indicated it again. ' – Deutschland.' He smiled at Klaus then looked at us once more.

'Deutschland – that's "Germany" in German. Now, does

anyone here speak German?' The boy who had sniggered before shouted out 'Ja, mein Herr' making us all laugh.

Klaus sat next to me. He didn't speak English but we managed somehow in Latin. He told me he had been born and brought up in Germany but when his father died his mother had married an Englishman. He had only been here a week but he liked it. He said that he and I were friends – amici sumus. That was nearly twenty years ago.

I really should get down to some work. Normally I work hard, very hard. In the name of Cochrane and Assocs. I deal in money: I buy it, sell it, lend it. I deal only with certain people and in private. They have confidence in me. They assume that having maintained credibility in the past then our house will do so in the future – and perhaps they are right, for as long as they trust us then we can do business and so justify that trust. In the course of time I am expected to become head of the firm. I would have liked that.

When I was a child our family was well off. There was an inheritance which my father employed wisely. I attended public school before going up to Oxford to read Classics. I was hard-working rather than brilliant. My father died when I was in my third year and I returned home immediately, to be told that he had committed suicide. We were completely bankrupt. Everything had to be sold; I had to leave Oxford and begin working in the City. For the last ten years I have worked hard to restore the family name.

Last night we had a special dinner, Sylvia and I, to celebrate our wedding anniversary – we have been married for five years. Afterwards she said she was proud of me as a husband, lover and merchant banker. She kissed me.

Recently I have had occasion to go over our company books and it has become apparent to me that our business methods are as hopelessly out-of-date as our furniture and fittings – and with our present commitments it is too late to correct the situation. We will be finished by the end of the year. Strictly speaking we are finished already but as yet no-one else knows. However, once word gets round the City, we will have to shut up shop, for a company that is failing, especially an old company, may inspire pity – but never investment. I want to tell my wife. I want to tell my partners.

Instead I say nothing. I stand at my office window staring out into the street at a complete stranger standing in the pouring rain. She has hardly moved from where I first saw her. She must be soaked through and very cold now. She appears very unhappy – I would like to go over and speak to her, to say 'Don't worry,' or something like that; or perhaps even just smile at her from here. I would like to, but I know I won't.

On his first night in our dormitory Klaus was given the bed next to mine and I could hear him crying. The room was in darkness but I could just make him out under the blankets. He was kneeling and bending forwards with his head pushing into the pillow.

'Klaus, Klaus,' I called in a low voice. Quietly I went over to him and sat on his bed.

'Don't cry, don't cry. You're here now. It will be good – you and me together. Honest.'

He made some reply in a voice muffled as much by his tears as by the blankets. He probably hadn't understood a word I had said. I sat with him for nearly half-an-hour while he cried, then I went back to bed. The next night was the same, and every night afterwards. During the day he was fine: he worked hard in class and joined in the games. Gradually his English improved. Each night, however, he cried himself to sleep. Then one day, during the morning break, he told me that from then on he was going to speak only in German – except to me, of course. At first I thought he was joking, but he wasn't.

The next class was arithmetic and near the end of the lesson our teacher began going over the problems out loud.

'Klaus, Number four please, the one about the reservoir.'

Klaus stood up to give his answer. He seemed uncertain and he mumbled. The teacher asked him to repeat it. He spoke more clearly this time:

'Zwei Minuten.' The class laughed and even the teacher joined in a little before asking him to repeat it in English.

'Zwei Minuten.' The class laughed even louder, but this time the teacher didn't even smile.

'In English, Klaus, if you please,' he said quite firmly.

'Zwei Minuten,' Klaus repeated; his fingers were gripping the sides of the desk-lid and his body shook. The teacher asked him again, and again the class went into uproar at his reply. His face was white. He was gripping the desk so tightly it rattled against the floor. He began repeating his answer: 'Zwei Minuten Zwei Minuten Zwei Minuten...' He was staring straight ahead quite oblivious to the noise about him.

The teacher didn't know what to do. He told Klaus to sit down and he wouldn't. To be quiet and he wouldn't. To stand in the corner and he wouldn't. 'Zwei Minuten Zwei Minuten....' Tears were running down his cheeks and his voice was choking but he couldn't stop. Finally he was taken to the sick-room.

He came back afterwards but still refused to speak English. A few days later he was sent home. I have never seen him since and hardly even given him a moment's thought until now.

It has stopped raining. The woman is still waiting there but in the sunlight she looks less miserable. She has been there for forty minutes now, at least.

To work. I suppose I have to fill up the day somehow and then return home. And I will have to think how to tell Sylvia that the business is collapsing.

She will have cooked dinner for my arrival tonight and we will eat together with the children. Afterwards I will read them a bedtime story, then we will probably watch TV. A few hours later it will be time to go to bed – and still I will not have told her.

And tomorrow I will return to the office; and the day after. There will be letters marked 'urgent', cables, meetings, luncheons, delicate negotiations and so forth. And every evening I will return home to Sylvia. Back and forwards; back and forwards I will go, saying nothing.

The woman has turned to check her appearance in the shop-window. She is adjusting her hat. I watch as she crosses the road and now walks quickly past my window and down the street.

I have sat down in my executive leather chair. At any moment the telephone may ring or my secretary announce someone to see me – until then I will do nothing except rest my feet on the desk. For how long? I wonder.

'Zwei Minuten Zwei Minuten....' I hear Klaus say.

The Doctor's Trip Downtown

The doctor promised there would be no pain but suddenly his finger-tips caught fire, and the green and gold flames burnt out my eyes. The pain woke me up – a pity really as I'm much less trouble when I'm asleep. I'm not all bad of course, but I'll be much worse now that I am blind.

'What difference does it make?' the doctor reassures me. 'Come on Bart, close your eyes and I'll give you some morphine.' His sensitive fingers feel for the small capillaries under my tongue because the rest of my veins have collapsed. He keeps on chatting so as to comfort me.

'Of course it's dark,' he tells me, 'It's the middle of the night, isn't it? Go back to sleep.' A harmless fiction I suppose; you can't blame him really, because I *am* a nuisance sometimes. Anyway he will give me some valium and that, crushed up in a shot of morphine, should keep me out of mischief for a while.

Sometimes I just lie on my bed snuffling and sobbing for hours. The doctor thinks that I enjoy it and that it is good for me – 'a good cry' is what he calls it and he thinks that I feel much better afterwards. He wants me to go to sleep now for it is time for him to make another of his trips downtown.

I really don't know why he bothers but every so often he starts getting nervy and jumpy and then off he goes. And it is the same old story every time – when he sees me again afterwards he always looks so dejected. There he goes! He's looking round at me and probably thinking to himself that my hand is twitching as I sleep, but actually I'm waving him good-bye.

As I said, it's the same old story every time. Let me tell you what will happen:

It will be snowing. A gang will be standing under a street-light in their shirt-sleeves. Over by some railings a fair-haired girl will be holding a broken bottle. The doctor used to think it would be noble to die for love, but now he thinks it would be nobler to kill for it. He smiles to himself as he remembers what he did last time he was here – how he promised the taxi-driver so much for each time round the block so he could watch the action develop, and how, when he was three pounds down and still nothing had happened, he got bored and gave up.

This time, however, he intends his trip downtown to be more successful; this time he has a much better plan. He always has a much better plan! This time he will get the driver to park directly opposite so that he has a perfect view of the gang. He is so sure of success that he probably won't even be afraid for if things do get out of hand he can always have the taxi driven off immediately.

There seems to be a bit of shoving and pushing going on. The doctor is getting restless, however, for the light is very poor and he isn't close enough to make out the details of skin-tension and diminishing pupil-size that are so crucial in fine judgements of this kind. He is convinced that to have any hope of success he must be fully aware of everything that happens exactly when it is happening. This, of course, is impossible.

Every time he returns I tell him that if he is going to succeed then it will be purely by luck. He doesn't know what he is expected to do or when he is expected to do it, but still he keeps trying. At each attempt he tries to eliminate further the element of chance and this is where I think he is making his big mistake. If he left everything to chance he may just succeed one time.

He demands a pair of field-glasses from the driver and watches the snow melt on the lips of one of the girls. With all the wind and snow it is difficult to hear what the men are shouting at each other so he winds down the window. Suddenly it is utterly silent. There are a few last snowflakes and everything is still.

Knowing that he has failed yet again he steps wearily out of the taxi and crosses the street to have a closer look so that he will know better next time. As usual the men are standing in deep snow; they are partially decayed and their shirt-sleeves hang tattered in the windless atmosphere. Thoroughly depressed once more, he is giving the snow a last futile kick when the girl with fair hair calls him to wait. As she approaches him she begins to grow smaller and younger, her voice becoming like a child's. Would he take her home? she asks.

The doctor takes her hand and brings her back to the taxi. She tells him that her name is Catherine, she is six years old. She explains that she was on her way home from school when she got lost. From the way that she is playing with the flip-up seats the doctor thinks that she has never been in a taxi before.

They move off through the deserted streets. Many of the shopfronts are smashed and the snow has drifted inside. There are burnt-out heaps of garbage and furniture; abandoned cars, buses and lorries. Everything is covered with snow. As the city centre appears to have been completely evacuated the doctor considers that even if Catherine could remember where she lived there is little point in taking her there. Meanwhile she has finished playing with the seats and is looking out of the window. The doctor has never been very good with children. He is afraid that she is going to burst into tears or throw a tantrum. However she gives a bored sigh and shrugs her shoulders then settles back in her seat.

The doctor thinks that the taxi is going too slowly and so he raps on the communicating glass; the driver ignores him. Suddenly a man lurches into the path of the headlights. It is me, but of course the doctor does not realise this. He has to bang furiously on the glass before the taxi will stop. I seem to be very drunk. For a moment I lean against the bonnet of the taxi then I stumble off into the darkness.

The doctor always gets very excited at this point.

'Follow him,' he shouts to the driver, and the taxi is turned round slightly to find me in the darkness. The snow is falling very thickly by this time and it is difficult to keep me in sight as I stumble this way and that. I keep falling down and struggling to my feet again until finally I seem to be down for good. The doctor orders the driver to stop and he gets out.

It is bitterly cold now and the doctor has to force his way against the wind to reach me where I sit hunched against an up-ended cooker. Despite the weather I am wearing only a thin summer suit, shirt and gym-shoes; I am shivering with cold and whimpering. The doctor has to brush away some of the snow before he recognises me.

'I might have guessed it would be you,' he says wearily and then shouts to the driver for help. The driver, of course, ignores him. Instead Catherine comes to help him carry me back into the taxi.

'This is Bart,' says the doctor when they bring me inside.

'Poor Bart, poor man,' Catherine repeats over and over again; she takes my hands in hers and begins rubbing them warm. I always like this. Then she puts her small arms round me and rocks me gently back and forth. I like this even better. Then the doctor raps on the window and the taxi moves off.

Gradually I appear to warm up and become more conscious. I start moaning again. The doctor, in sheer exasperation, lights a cigarette and begins staring determinedly out of the window.

Catherine wants to amuse me and so she starts making faces at me – the silly girl hasn't yet realised that I'm blind. She becomes confused by my lack of response so she taps me on the cheek. I immediately start whimpering louder than before. She looks across to the doctor who appears to be doing his best to ignore both of us. Finally she gives a sigh and settles back in her seat.

But only for a moment, for she begins tugging at her hair. She is about to say something. Quite suddenly she sits up straight.

'I know what,' she announces, 'I'll tell you a story – not a made up story but a real one that I was in once.' I whimper at her encouragingly; the doctor looks at her for a moment then continues staring out of the window. Catherine begins her story.

'Once upon a time when I was in the Sudan I was dressed up in the clothes of a princess. There were satins and silks so fine that when you threw them up into the air they floated down slowly and almost perfectly flat. There were perfumes for different parts of my body and for different times of the day; there were precious stones that seemed on fire.'

Catherine stops telling her story as tears are beginning to run down her face. I reach for her and take her on my knee to comfort her. The doctor remains looking out of the window. I do my best to cheer her up by tickling her and whispering nonsense to her. Soon she responds, her face is flushed and she is squealing with laughter.

'He's a doctor,' I tell her.

'I thought so,' she replies with contempt.

The doctor, however, appears to be remaining aloof from all this by looking out of the window. Suddenly Catherine has caught his eye, for he has not been looking out of the window at all but at her reflection in the glass. She returns his stare as she slides her hand inside my shirt and begins stroking my chest. She is singing softly.

The taxi picks up speed now and the doctor begins to get worried. It is being driven very carelessly – no sooner colliding with something than it accelerates off again almost immediately, skidding from side to side in the snow. In fact the doctor gets quite scared and raps on the glass, shouts and stamps on the floor. The driver ignores him. Catherine continues to sing softly and I sit holding her hand.

When the taxi hits a stationary bus the doctor makes an attempt to jump out, but is much too slow. He has become so terrified he no longer knows if Catherine and I are inside or outside him; whether he is a fair-haired girl standing by some railings or a blind man wandering in the snow. The taxi leaves the road to plunge its passengers to certain death.

Each of the doctor's trips downtown ends like this. And yet, he returns to tell only of a summer's afternoon and of a sky so blue as to be almost without colour. He sits on the edge of my bed and begins:

'Firstly, let us consider how sunlight spills from out of our cupped hands.' – And, as always, he promises there will be no pain.

A Private Joke

Whoever Christine has become she keeps secret. I say to her, 'We are still friends,' pausing to ask a moment later, 'Aren't we?' Her appearance has changed: she wears smarter clothes, more jewelry, and her hair is cropped close. Whenever we meet nowadays I am uncertain how to behave. I become self-concious and find it difficult to concentrate on our conversation. Sometimes I catch a glimpse of the woman I knew previously in her pronunciation of certain words and in her laughter. Otherwise I hardly know her.

It is nearly midnight and she is asleep on the bed. I am standing at the window looking down onto the stream of refugees making its way slowly through the town. They move almost soundlessly through the falling snow; the old people sitting on carts when possible, or else walking as best they can. At the edge of the town there is a large camp where they can stay for two nights and receive food, a chance to rest, to wash clothes – then they must move on. The next camp is four days' journey.

I live on the third storey of a block of flats and quite often I find myself standing here looking at the men and women trudging past with their belongings. I am rather drunk at the moment and am leaning my forehead against the cold glass. Christine is mumbling in her sleep. I will go across to her, lie beside her again. On the way over to the bed I upset a small table with flowers on it. The vase falls to the floor and smashes. She wakes momentarily to ask, 'Is that you Francis?' and is immediately asleep again. When I try to close my eyes I feel dizzy and sick. When I open them I see the glare of the snow reflected against the ceiling and walls. Towards morning I wake to find she has gone.

Two letters have arrived. Neither is addressed to me – I feel there is little chance these days of a letter reaching its intended destination. The first is very short: Dear Raymond, it begins. The shoes. I should like the yellow shoes. You know why. Love Marion. The other letter is mostly accusations that Sylvia is seeing too much of 'a certain party' very close to the writer. It has been written in anger. Then accusations continue tediously – then I receive a sudden jolt when I read that the certain party is called Maurice, like myself. I begin to read with more interest but quite abruptly the tone changes: the topic drifts to the refugees, to travel in general, holidays – and in conclusion the hope is expressed that a visit might be arranged in the near future.

I finish breakfast standing at the window drinking coffee. The roadway is covered in slush and resembles a river flowing grey-black between banks of heaped-up dirty snow. As the weather has cleared I can hear the men and women coughing and calling to each other. I decide to do some work.

Nowadays it is considered old-fashioned to compose at the piano, but recently I have felt the need to hear the sounds I am imagining, otherwise I tend to lose the thread of my own argument. Picking up the manuscript I am working on at present I think to myself, what does this sound like? These marks that I have made – these erasures, corrections and further erasures, what are they? I play a few of the more easily discernible bars trying to recognise something.

The doorbell rings. It is Stanley, one of my students. His face is glowing red with the cold and he is smiling. What does he want? A lesson. It seems that I promised him a lesson. A piano lesson? Composition? I have forgotten which. He is going over to the piano – good, I can just sit and listen, commenting every so often. But he is taking handwritten sheets from his bag. I should say to him – I cannot listen to your music, not today. I should make some excuse: say that I am unwell, but instead I bring another chair to the piano and ask him to begin.

Perhaps when Christine came last night I should have told her I was unwell – she may have asked me to lie down; she may have offered to massage me gently as she used. At least she would have spared me the lecture on her marriage and how good it is now –

thanks to my tender and unique friendship; thanks to my sensitivity and understanding which helped her through that difficult period of her 'temporary psychosis' – a new and particularly fatuous expression she repeated several times during the evening. She was 'AOK' now, and the drunker she became the more frequently and emphatically she reassured me of the fact.

Shouting has begun outside and Stanley has stopped playing. He is looking at me. I look closely at the score. I compliment him on his interpretation. Suddenly there is a scream from outside. Stanley gets up and rushes to the window.

'The bastards!' he shouts. 'Just look at them will you,' he says turning to me. I go over to the window.

Outside, the stream of refugees has met with an obstruction: there is a confused crowd of people and carts spreading across the street and pushing those at the edge up onto the banks of snow. In the centre, men, women and police are fighting. Several people are lying on the road.

'The bastards. The bastards,' Stanley repeats loudly. Gradually everything quietens down. Those who seem hurt are put onto the carts and the rest begin trudging once more in the direction of the camp. Stanley says that he cannot talk to me about his music just now. He seems very agitated. 'As you please,' I reply. Then he asks if he can come back tomorrow. I would like to say no – instead I agree and suggest that he leaves me the score so that I can examine it in greater detail.

When Stanley has gone I look at my own composition once more. I pick it up and play through a few bars. I gaze out of the window then play through a few more bars; make some erasures then some coffee. I look out of the window for a while, glance through the score once again. Then I decide to go for a walk.

While getting my coat from the bedroom I notice some children playing out in the back court. They are making snowmen – gigantic snowmen, some of them over seven feet tall that with their gross features look grotesque, like giant children.

The stair-lights have failed again so the corridor and stair-well are in near darkness. Someone comes up to me, he seems to be heavily built. 'I will take you down,' he says. He switches on a torch and together we walk downstairs – the lift has been out of order ever since the steel pulleys were requisitioned.

'Out of the way you,' he says roughly to some people who are huddling on the steps. And further down: 'Out of the way for the Professor,' he orders, kicking another who is asleep. Why should I trust him any more than people who are fast asleep? I wonder to myself as I follow him downstairs. When we reach the street I give him some change, he thanks me and goes inside again.

What a noise there is here! The refugees trudge past taking up the entire width of the road so that every few moments I am forced to step into heaps of snow to let them go by. I turn down the first side-street.

These quiet, prosperous streets would be empty but for the abandoned vehicles; the houses are barricaded with planks and sheets of corrugated iron. I stop for a moment to look at one of the gardens, trying to imagine how it is laid out under the snow. I think I can discern where the lawn is, and the flower-beds. To get a closer view I am leaning over the wall when I catch sight of someone at an upstairs window. I move on.

It must be mid-afternoon now and I am still walking. Quite unexpectedly I see Christine at the side-door of one of the houses, she beckons to me and I am let in.

This then is the stage-set for the newly perfected marriage. There is no furniture; the floor is uncarpeted, the shutters closed. In an open fire I see gilded picture-frames burning, torn books and wads of photographs curling in the heat. She apologises for everything: she tried to tell me last night, but couldn't. She is going to leave when her husband returns. I should leave too, she adds. Can't I see what is happening?

Why don't I take her in my arms now, kiss her tenderly? I think to myself – say to her, 'Come and live with me instead. I will protect you, I will love you. The rest does not concern us.'

Would I leave with her this evening? she asks. While we still can. I take her hand and hold it.

'Maurice,' she says firmly, 'will you leave with us this evening?' I do not know what to reply. I kiss her.

'There will be several of us going, do you understand?'

She has not responded to my kiss; her fingers brush my cheek then she smiles. She tells me where we shall meet and what I should bring. We say goodbye in the cold hallway. Please come with us, she urges. I promise that I will.

Darkness is falling as I make my way home to pack. Passing a bar, I go in to have a brandy then, realising that I have not eaten since breakfast, I order some sandwiches. They will be brought over to my table, says the barman, indicating a nearby seat. While waiting I have another brandy.

Christine is right: any day now civil law will break down completely – it requires greater and greater force to sustain it. Yet hardly anyone leaves. How normal the bar looks now –

'Professor!' I recognise Stanley's voice. He is coming over to me from the bar, his face flushed even more red than usual. He is smiling broadly; I will say that I am about to leave. My sandwiches arrive.

'You can't sit here all by yourself – come over and join us.'

'No, really Stanley, thank you but I—'

'It's my birthday! Come on, what are you drinking?' And before I can stop him, he has picked up my glass and is holding it to his nose.

'And another brandy!' he calls to the barman.

I follow Stanley to an already overcrowded table – he with a tray of drinks, I with my plate of sandwiches. He introduces me.

'My professor, the celebrated composer and pianist, Maurice Dryden.'

Several more brandies. The girl sitting next to me has long yellow hair and she is called Liz.

The snowmen were so large, easily seven feet tall and child-like. They looked sub-normal, do you understand?

Oh yes, moronic snowmen, she replies.

And the children were building them so very seriously, carrying armloads of snow from all over the yard then standing on each other's shoulders to reach up high.

I think I'd like another drink, she says. I kiss her, knowing the moment is perfect, seeing Liz lean towards me to offer me a cigarette, knowing we shall sleep together tonight. Christine is leaving now, she is saving herself and others from the collapse of civil law.

Liz is still leaning towards me. She will kiss me. Her hair brushes my cheek. Closing my eyes I see snow falling in the dark streets: an image in black and white of footsteps and silence. Barricades that disintegrate like charred paper.

Her warm breath, her lips. I see soldiers and refugees raising the dead only to let them freeze in the open streets.

Her tongue touches mine.

The snow falls onto the roadway. Liz is holding onto my arm. We begin to walk unsteadily. Falling and helping each other up again. Leaning against walls and heaps of snow. Until torchlight shines into my eyes.

I look away and another torch is switched on. We stand still. We give them our money, our watches, our jewellery. When the torches are switched off we stumble into the darkness turning left and right through the snow.

So many refugees and so wretched. You are nearly at the camp now, I reassure them. There is a small boy clutching an umbrella. He walks as if he is asleep. You're sleep-walking, I say to him with a smile. Liz is trying to pull me back. I am going to give him some money for sweets, I tell her, beginning to go through my pockets.

A man comes over and gives the boy a shove sending him into the middle of the stream of refugees. The boy has done nothing wrong, I protest. Listen, I say to him grabbing his arm, I wanted to give him some money for sweets, that's all.

The man tries to shake himself free.

Do you deny him even that? I demand.

Then he turns to me and says something – but I cannot understand him.

Of course! I should have realised, and he will not have understood a word I've been saying to him, nor will the boy. Everything's alright now; I smile at him and wave over to the boy. I understand their mistrust, and I don't mind. No hard feelings.

I reach to shake his hand to show that despite everything we can still part in friendship. He shoves me into the snow.

Next morning I am standing at the window. The refugees are still filing past and soldiers have been posted every few yards along the road to ensure that they keep moving. While I have been away my flat has been broken into: drawers emptied onto the floor; books and papers torn-up and scattered everywhere; furniture overturned.

The doorbell is ringing. Someone walks in claiming she is Christine. She asks if I am alright.

'We waited for you,' she says. 'The van is outside but you must come now or it will be too late.' She is wearing a man's coat and muffler – her face is very pale. 'Just leave all this; come as you are,' she says jokingly.

'I can manage,' I reply. 'You go on down and I will be with you in a few moments.'

Some time later I am woken by the sound of gunfire and muffled explosions. The street outside is deserted except for men running from doorway to doorway shooting at each other. Sometimes one of them falls in the snow.

Several people have come out from the shop opposite with their hands in the air. One of them is Stanley. Although his face is smeared with blood and dirt I can still recognise him. There is a quick burst of machine-gun fire and he falls to the ground.

'The bastards,' I shout out loud. 'The bastards!' I rush out of the flat and force my way down the crowded stairs in the darkness, pushing and kicking people aside until I reach the street-door.

'I must get out,' I say to the people there. 'You must let me out – one of my students, a friend of mine, has been shot and he's lying out there in the snow.'

'Leave him,' they reply '– or the soldiers will come in here and kill us as well.'

I plead with them until eventually they say they will let me pass. One of them however, makes it clear that I will not be allowed back in, adding, 'not under any circumstances.'

I agree to this and very cautiously the door is opened. Then, when there is enough room, someone shoves me in the back so that I stumble out into the middle of the road.

The sun is shining brightly and the snow dazzles.

'Get back in there,' a voice shouts. I look up the street: a man is pointing a machine-gun straight at me.

'I wanted to-' I begin.

'Hands on your head,' comes another voice opposite. I do as I am told and stand as still as I can, but I have begun to tremble with the cold.

'My friend-' I begin again, indicating Stanley, 'he-'

'He is dead,' interrupts the man opposite. 'Now get back into that house.'

I begin the return to the street door – perhaps they will let me back in as I am alone. I turn the handle but it is jammed. I hammer on the door with my fists but there is no reply.

Perhaps if I walk back towards the man with the gun; if I explain to him I care only for my friend lying in the snow; if I can make him understand that the rest is really not my concern....

Then out of the corner of my eye I see Stanley wink at me. And all at once the sound of someone's laughter seems to fill the entire street – it even rattles the barricades. I feel it begin in my stomach, then spread throughout my body until I am shaking helplessly. I have gone weak in the knees and fallen into the snow where I roll around unable to stop laughing.

Stanley is lying close to me, quite still. He smiles at me, I smile back. A private joke.

2

The Story of
The Imaginary Horse

When both my parents were dead I returned to the family house.
It was understood that I should remain here for the rest of my life
looked after by the gardener and his wife, the housekeeper. Of
the two the latter is more terrifying. At night she patrols the
corridors, flourishing a candelabra and listening for me. Am I
asleep? Have I taken all my medicines, my injections?

Up and down the stairs, across the landings, the East wing, the
West wing she goes checking the windows, the cupboards and
the keyholes. Indiscreetly close I follow her, imitating everything
she does – sometimes even managing to catch the slight side to
side slouch that has taken her kind generations to regress to.
When she scratches so do I, and we spit almost in unison...She
never glances backwards, perhaps she can't.

Later in the evening I often stand at the bottom of the main
stairs listening to the two of them down in the kitchen, eating,
drinking and grunting at each other in their border dialect. What
can they find to talk about – day after day they see only me and
the rain?

Every three months, however, a lawyer comes to pay their
wages and deal with the accounts. I no longer receive him. He is
accompanied by a small polite man, my doctor, who, even when
the fun (more of this later) is at its most fast and furious, never
fails in the respect due to a private patient.

I have two responses to him – either I face the wall and remain
utterly passive, answering in positive monosyllables: Yes, I am
happy; Yes, I am in good health; Yes, I have a good appetite; Yes,
I go my walk every day. This is my October and April response –
until the fun starts, of course. – Or else, as in January and July, I
am pleasant, affable and cooperative. On these occasions I play
the genial, enlightened host – one educated gentleman

encountering another in a barbarous country. I discourse in an elegant mélange of English and French, promoting a conversation whose brilliancy must surely recall his youthful ambitions to be something other than the country quack he has become. And sooner or later during these visits I begin to tell the story of the imaginary horse.

Dull though my doctor is, experience has made him suspicious – a local virtue. So subtly now do I begin the telling, laying the scene and the circumstances almost imperceptibly around my innocent listener, that the story is already far advanced before this provincial sawbones has realised what is happening.

What betrays me? Is it my eyes, or do I grip the chair-back with a too-sudden and embarrassing tenacity? Perhaps my worldly manner overwhelms him. – Whatever, all at once this small-time, small-town, medicine-man becomes alarmed and calls to the housekeeper and her husband who loiter in attendance, dragging their knuckles by the door.

And that's when the fun really starts – after all, having waited three months for this I intend making the most of it. Chairs and foot-stools go flying; lamps (there is no electricity here) sail across the room trailing an oily-coloured paraffin rainbow; books and vases are hurled playfully from side to side; window-panes shatter. The brutes, with their witchdoctor-vet coming a poor third, shamble after me knocking over furniture and tangling themselves in the curtains. Everyone is shouting at the top of his voice and no-one is listening. I continue relating the story as best I can, screaming out loud to be heard above the din.

But all too soon I'm forced onto the ground and held there, weeping and defeated. The housekeeper is on top of me – she is all motherly compassion, sweat and herring-breath. Her husband frets at one side then cautiously bends down to place his folded jacket under my head. My sleeve is rolled up. A swift dab of antiseptic – then blankness. A heaviness that takes days to pass. I wake up howling with the effort to remember who and where I am.

A certain turning on the stairs, a cupboard-shelf, the step

down into the kitchen – when I was a child these parts of the house were charged with significance. Soon there remained only my growing vocabulary and the memory of one place and one moment. What symmetry is being played out now?

After I have been ill, which I confess is not just when the doctor calls, a woman with calm eyes comes to look after me. She feeds me, cleans me and sometimes, for a few precious moments each day, takes my head to rest against her beating heart. She does this to remind herself that I am human. Occasionally the housekeeper and her husband look in, grimace their encouragement, and withdraw.

In the mornings I am taken to the window and left there; in the evenings a battery TV is wheeled forward and a channel-switch placed in my hand. When I hear someone's approach along the corridor I turn it on and look straight ahead. It is the least I can do.

Over twenty years have passed since I returned to the family home. By now the pattern of sickness and recovery is so well established, and so pitiless, that once again – as in my earliest childhood – I sense there is only one place and one moment. Perhaps I shall die as I was born – among strangers, and unmoved by any suffering other than my own.

Who first told me the story of the imaginary horse? I remember being in a room with white-painted walls and a large bay-window looking into the garden where sunlight was burning itself out in autumn colours. I am certain I was by myself yet someone's voice began coaxing me to place my ear against the polished wooden floor, to listen, they said, for the hoofbeats of a distant and imaginary horse.

Enough, no more memories. Not now when life is far too urgent a matter. Reminiscence is excusable when one is younger and still half-asleep – when even a ten-mile walk, let alone climbing the stairs, is taken for granted.

The fact is, I am getting too old for all these quarterly high jinks, a treat though they are. Also, small details of the story keep slipping from my mind – not the broad outline, there is no danger of that, not yet. I suspect that the local ju-ju man, my only audience so far, is quite insensitive to such matters as internal coherence; nevertheless, if I do not make this one effort at writing it down I fear the story might soon become no more than a series of unrelated lies.

It certainly isn't the same, sitting here calmly at my desk with the afternoon sunlight gently illuminating sheet after sheet of exercise-paper. The only sound is my turning the page every so often as I continue with my patient work. Rather a change from the more customary accompaniment of smashing wood and screams of despair. However in these trying and tranquil circumstances I do the best I can.

And what's that? They're banging on the door. I locked it so I would not be disturbed – but here they are, turning the handle this way and that, hammering their fists (*that's* the housekeeper's and *that's* her husband's) on the heavy panels.

They're whining and raging out there. All that noise, and they expect to be let in! At last, after God only knows how many years, I've managed a few moment's peace and quiet to set down a story, *one* story, and all this starts.

I'll fire them! That's what I'll do, send them packing. I'll live in the kitchen myself and do my entertaining there. I'll send out invitations to all my former friends – I still have their addresses – and to the various up-and-coming artists, diplomats, scientists and so on I might wish to recognise.

I'll create a salon here in the wilderness. One that will be the envy of all Europe. One that will make Mmes. de Staël, du Barry and the rest sit up and rub their sockets with astonishment. I may even marry. – Do you hear that, you quadrupeds out there! I may even marry. Where would you be then?

But soon it will be too late. The door will have given way and everything will be back to normal. Back to the screaming and roaring. Back to running round the room shouting at the tops of our voices. To speed things up I'll make a paper-chase from these heaps of A4.

Then we'll be off. There goes a lamp-shade, there a wooden elephant, a bookcase, and now a piece of Dresden.

What fun! But all too soon it will be over again. All too soon they will capture me and force me to the ground. I will be kicking and biting as they roll up my sleeve. I will be weeping.

As the heaviness descends it will take all of them to hold me down, for it is then that the bay-window opens and the colours of the garden enter the room one by one. Only the imaginary horse will be shut out. And I alone, my head pressed hard against the polished wooden floor, will be forced to hear its hoofbeats as it gallops back and forth in terror.

Rehearsals for First Love

For Sharon I created a colour between sky-blue and sea-blue when, half-asleep one winter's morning, I could still feel a young girl's arms around me – her arms. How else can I describe falling in love for the first time?

By drawing my fingernail across the glass I made the frost crack. When I traced out the letters of her name, they soon disappeared – to return with each morning's frost, written in that colour lying between sunlight and ice.

This evening I am being driven home through the West End where the shoplights give out a yellowish glare in the early darkness. We turn down Wardour Street. The pavements are crowded, filthy. Surely there is someone here who will come when my chauffeur calls her over to climb into the car and sit close to me; someone who will be called 'Sharon'. She promised we would meet again.

The ringing of the garage bell announced her. I got up from doing my homework and went round to the pumps where a Cresta was standing.

'Fill her up,' says the driver. The girl sitting beside him makes a remark and he laughs. Then he turns to me.

'What are you waiting for?' he asks. The girl had blonde hair.

'The keys – for the petrol cap,' I reply in embarrassment. Through the near window I look at the girl, then look away again – she is watching me all the time, trying to catch my eye.

'That's her full now,' I call out a few minutes later.

'Feels nice,' sighs the girl rubbing herself against the back of the seat. Then when he hands over a pound-note she asks, 'Aren't you going to give him something?'

'There should be threepence over,' the man explains, adding, 'of course you'd give him something else, wouldn't you?'

'Wouldn't I just!' she replies smiling at me. I know I should go back to the garage now, but I don't move.

The man asks, 'Would you rather have threepence from me, or something else from Sharon here?' They both look at me. They are waiting for a reply. Eventually I stammer '– something from Sharon.'

'Then you will have to give me back my threepence first.' Hurriedly I search through my overalls and find a threepenny piece. Then I wait.

The man starts the engine and shouts, 'Ta-ra.' Sharon smiles at me as she winds up the window. Then she winks.

'Next time we meet-' she promises as the car drives off.

'Stop!' I call out suddenly to my chauffeur, 'I think I saw someone back there at the last set of lights.' Regardless of the traffic he does a U-turn then leans over and opens the window to call her over. The girl looks up and approaches my car. She is wearing a yellow suit. While they are talking I examine her carefully – every so often she glances towards me but I know she cannot see anything through the tinted glass.

After a few minutes I come to a decision. It is a case of mistaken identity, very mistaken – the voice and the deportment are all wrong. I tap twice on the communicating glass and the car is immediately driven off.

Her smile and her light-blue eyes excepted, Sharon's appearance belongs to another time. I realise that her clothes, her make-up, her hair-style and her vocabulary would seem very old-fashioned, perhaps even comical, if I actually saw them in the street. But back in my flat these are easily restored.

The chauffeur drives slowly. Every so often I ask him to stop for a few moments – it is getting quite dark and unless they are standing in full light, which they almost never do, I am unable to see them clearly.

When I find a suitable girl we shall go to my flat where everything has been prepared. The piano lid is raised; there are a few books scattered on the window-seat; a print hangs above the fireplace. I do not understand why, but small details seem to change every time. Of one item, however, I am certain: this print.

It is the very print that once hung in Sharon's house.

I bought it a few years ago when some of the family property came up for public auction after her father's death. It is a plan of the original estate. The rooms, outhouses and gardens are labelled in neat script; field workers and other servants – drawn rather out of proportion to the buildings – are set in their proper locations. To present a complete picture of the estate it was necessary that as one gardener is shown planting rose-bushes so another is seen selecting and cutting the full blooms; as one group (a family portrait, perhaps) is skating on the frozen pond to the left of the house so, on the other side, the same group is playing tennis.

Another certainty is how I shall feel when I see this girl enter the room – even though I will not go to kiss nor to take her hand. As she comes towards me I will watch her reflection in the glass overlaying the print. Then I will turn to face her.

And so unconditional, so overwhelming will be my response to her at that moment that she will at once exist too deep within me to imagine her, anymore than I can imagine myself. Her smile, the way she will hold her cigarette, how her fingertips will smooth back her long blonde hair – all these actions will be performed, exactly as directed, by whatever girl I take home with me. And yet, in each of these gestures I will perceive something of Sharon; and through them discover others more secret, belonging to us alone.

At last I have found someone suitable. After a few moments I offer her a cigarette; as she takes it she says something in reply, makes a joke. And immediately I am painfully reminded that even this short opening scene is merely another rehearsal. Still, she is quite pretty and, what is more, I think her appearance can be made close enough to Sharon's to deceive me at odd moments. Perhaps even Sharon, however, was herself never more than the understudy for another who had become too much a part of me ever to receive my love. Realising this, I understand something of how my love for Sharon, though long past, can still fill me with longing and regret.

Before I can stop her, the girl beside me has gone on to tell me that her name is Caroline and she likes big cars.

'Your name is Sharon,' I manage to interrupt, 'and for this evening you will please wear this,' I continue, giving her a necklace of pale stones – jewellery to match the colour of her eyes. The colour I created. She smiles knowingly at me as she fastens the clasp behind her neck. The chauffeur drives us quickly home.

Sharon did not recognise me immediately. I had been invited to stay for the weekend by her brother who introduced us before briefly going upstairs to tell the rest of the family of my arrival.

'But of course!' she pretended when I took this opportunity to remind her how we had already met. 'You are the boy who *served* me that day in the garage, aren't you?' Then she offered me a drink.

'I will fill it right up,' she said, winking at me. When she handed me the glass her fingertips brushed against mine; when she explained the print of the house I could feel her pressing close to me. At dinner she whispered that she would come to my room later when everyone else would be asleep. Our love-making seemed to last only a few moments even as we heard the downstairs clock chime distinctly each hour.

'A few moments.' There have been so many other moments indistinguishable from these. For a long time now, whenever I have said to someone, 'I love you,' I have had to force myself to imagine a future for us – for only by anticipating some such imaginary future can I give my words any significance. Otherwise, making love, declaring love and even being in love are merely the casual acts and clichés, the everyday habits of a grown man.

There is no need to speak to the girl sitting beside me, she will be given her instructions when we arrive at my flat. My hand, however, rests in hers and she squeezes it from time to time. The conversation we shall have, the glitter of cutlery and plate, her perfume, her hair, her breath – all these dissolve around me whenever I feel the pressure of this hand. But shortly she will be made to learn by heart certain words of affection, certain loving gestures and caresses. Every action and phrase, every sensation will be gone over in the hope that the entire scene will be performed perfectly, for even now there are moments that can still move me profoundly – moments of rare and precious deception.

We have arrived. While she is being dressed, made-up and told what will be expected of her, I make sure everything is in place: the piano over by the window, books scattered nearby, the print hanging straight. Just before I press the bell that will summon her I go over to the window where the letters of her name have been scratched on the glass. For a few seconds, before the condensation of my breath evaporates from the pane, I read the name, 'Sharon'.

When she enters the room I feel shy, nervous that things will not go well; that I will forget what to do and what to say.

She asks me if I would like a drink. As she gives me the glass I notice that her hand is trembling slightly. Perhaps she is nervous also. I smile reassuringly. She draws my attention to the print then comes and stands close to me.

Everything seems exactly right, even the scent of her skin. Soon we will lie naked in each other's arms drenched in the colour I created for her: the sun will shine warmly on us and when we wish it, the moon also. Yet each time we kiss I long instead to say her name aloud.

The Tilting Room

This room is really known only to you and me. At least I think that's true, for I've not noticed that anyone else seems aware of what's happening here.

It's got many corners, hasn't it? And crevices? I'm sure that the walls and floors don't quite meet at right angles so that everything seems to tilt this way and that; ashtrays look as if they are about to slide off the table, books as if they are about to fall off the shelves. But, as you said when we moved in, it's just the way we see things and we should soon get used to it.

Well, you were quite right, for we got completely used to it and have stayed here for a long time now. The months and the years passed and our friends all met each other and got married. But we stayed put knowing when we were well off, didn't we? Of course we had to see their houses, gardens, garages and children, all on their best behaviour and planned with due regard to proportion and appearance as well-balanced families! But how glad we were at the end of the evening's socialising to climb to the very top of the stairs and at last enter our funny-shaped tilting room!

Goodness knows what we talked about for all these years, or what we did. Do you remember how every winter we sealed the windows against the wind and rain, then dragged and pushed the furniture up the floor's slope towards the fire? And there we sat for months on end drinking tea and talking, and having friends round and drinking more tea. Everyone was perched on chairs that seemed either to be about to pitch them onto the floor, or be so angled that the occupant would need to be helped out of it at the end of his visit. Inside our room tea drinking once more became an art form! Those were happy, happy days, perhaps they will return; I hope so.

You said that when Janice came back to stay with you it was like entering the room for the first time again. Once more you noticed that everything was askew. She said, 'Goodness,' and that next day everything would be tidied up and put in order. And first thing the next morning Janice began in earnest, nailing things up here and measuring things over there. And soon I hardly recognised what was, after all, my home. I was hoping that we would all get on well together, but now even you and I are hardly at ease with each other.

Yet there was a time when we tried, you and I, to involve her in our conversations. These were almost the last times that we talked together. It might have worked, only it didn't – and we know who the weak link was, don't we? And I thought things were going to work out so well too. At first she smiled and seemed to be listening, and then she laughed once or twice which was a good sign. I agree she looks very attractive when she smiles, who doesn't? So, she looks more than just attractive to you. That was obvious, spare me the excuses, I understand, really I understand.

But when she lies sleeping in your arms, sometimes, for a few moments in the small hours, I can feel the room see-sawing once more; and to keep my feet I must dance at the very least! Then I can sing you such tales, tell you such bedtime stories as will make your toes curl even as you sleep!

Talk to me! I'm not really bothered what we talk about, but you're the only person who can really talk to me just as I'm the only person who can really talk to you. So talk to me. Don't sit there looking at the titles of books or even reading them; don't pretend you're interested in what she's saying because I know you're not. It's all pretend isn't it? Talk to me, say it's all pretend. I thought we might talk sometimes when she'd gone out, I was hoping we might have a few words together at least, even just for old time's sake. But no; I feel as if you are about to speak to me sometimes, but instead you seem to think better of it and switch on the stereo or pick up a book.

After father died, remember how mother would switch on the radio the moment she was by herself? I'm certain she wasn't interested in what was being said, but as soon as she went off to make tea, or even go to the toilet, then on would go the radio broadcasting about beef yield, Concorde, someone's reminiscences or whatever. At first I assumed that she just wanted the company of a talking voice, but after a while I realised that this wasn't the case. Indeed it seemed that sometimes I would irritate her merely by being there, and then off she'd go to the kitchen saying she'd some tidying to do, and on would go the radio. What she wanted, I think, was to be unable to have to look at her thoughts; and so the radio was a continuous voice, a stream of consciousness that just drifted on effortlessly, bearing her with it. That the content did not involve her, or refer to her in any way was all to the good, as then the stream flowed for her without any personal obstruction.

Well so much for mother, except that you are getting like that now. Not that you listen to the radio all day, but that you make sure you do not have to listen to me as it were. You make sure that you don't have to think or even look at your thoughts. Up in the morning and read the Shreddies packet over breakfast, then shave with the radio on – you hardly ever do anything without the stereo playing, 'just to fill in the background,' you say. But it's not, is it? It's the foreground you're filling up, while in the background your body performs whatever actions are required, like eating or putting up shelves, quite automatically.

It's all the same to you really, whether it's Boccherini, butter mountains, Concorde or Shreddies packets, though I've put them in alphabetical order which is the same as any other order really, to you. Like the broadcasters, what you're afraid of is not whether what is being broadcast (the shreddies-butter mountain-Concorde and so on in your case) is uninteresting or uninformative, but simply that it might stop, even just for a moment. A kind of silent gap in eternity that, though it lasts only a few seconds, seems to partake of that eternity itself. Broadcasters call it 'dead time'.

And you're dead scared of dead time, of those gaps in eternity when we might talk to one another, aren't you? Perhaps you are sitting in the room that's neat and tidy now; you're listening to some Bach fugues, and you're trying to listen so hard, aren't you? Only nowadays you cannot listen to them, not even just one, all the way through without your mind starting to wander, trying to seek me out. And then you become not merely frightened, but terrified of the vast gap in eternity that may be just about to open up and leave you so very much alone, and with me only. So you take up a score of the fugue and between the two of them, the music and the score, you manage to hold together what you know is always, at any moment, just about to fall apart.

But don't worry, for I shall be with you at all times, and I am waiting for you to come through that gap to join me, should you ever let it open. Recently you have started taking pills so that you sleep deeply and dreamlessly; but tonight you were tired weren't you? Tonight you said you had no need of any pills. And so tonight while you are asleep I shall tell you a bedtime story. Perhaps you have heard some of it before, some of it may seem familiar to you. As I'm telling it to you, you will be wondering if it is a true story, but only you will know that. I call this story, 'An evening at home.' Are you sleeping comfortably? Then I'll begin.

You believe you are entering a room: a woman comes forward to greet you, she is smiling. 'You look tired,' she says, 'come and sit down beside me'.

Look round the room: as you can see, it's full of people, mostly strangers – some of them are eating at the table, some are watching TV or reading or talking. A group of children are playing ludo in front of the fire.

You sit down beside the woman, it is Janice, and you are just about to ask her who all those people are when one of the children, a girl of about thirteen or fourteen with fair hair, freckles, and a bandage on her knee, comes over to the settee to ask Janice if she would like play at ludo. Janice thanks her but says no, and smiles at the children who then shout over that perhaps you'd like to play instead? You reply that you would but you're too tired just now – at this they all shake their heads very seriously for a moment, and then laugh and call their friend to come back and get on with the game.

And now you notice, for the first time, a couple who are sitting on an armchair to the left of the fire. The woman is on the man's knee and he is lightheartedly kissing first her left hand, then her right hand, and then what must be an especially ticklish area at the side of her neck, for you can see that she giggles each time he kisses her there. They are not in the least embarrassed by all the people in the room, and when they do become aware of your staring at them so impolitely, it is you who feel uncomfortable. At this they break out into peals of laughter. The man, patting the woman affectionately on her knee, asks you if, after fifty years together, it is so surprising that they are still happy with one another? Rather awkwardly you assure him that it isn't. You are about to lie to him to explain why you were staring, when you notice that he is completly ignoring you again and is devoting his whole attention to that especially sensitive area mentioned before, making the woman giggle continuously. However, so as not to seem impolite at her companion's suddenly breaking off his conversation with you, she manages at the same time as being kissed to wave you a kind of goodbye over her partner's shoulder.

Janice is pouring you a drink and saying that you will need it for she has something very important to say. You take a sip of it and wait. She lights a cigarette.

'Well,' she begins, exhaling the smoke slowly, 'are you sitting comfortably?' You say that you are, and smile encouragingly.

'Well,' she continues, 'it would seem that you are about to become a father.'

There is a moment of total silence, and then the room is in an uproar as tables and chairs are pushed aside and everyone in the room, excepting you and Janice, rises to their feet and gives three cheers. Then all together they come over to you and begin a very confused and friendly procedure of hand shaking and back slapping, while the children do a dance round and round the settee. The two of you are sitting there like a king and queen being courted and entertained. You give everyone a drink.

Now that the announcement has been made and the last toast has just been drunk, you are hoping that all these people will finally go away and leave the two of you alone. However, you are disappointed to see that the ludo game is being resumed; those watching TV return to their seats; those at table take their places once again; in short, everyone settles down to spend a comfortable evening once more. Rather baffled by this behaviour you turn to Janice and say somewhat peevishly, 'You might have waited until we were all alone.'

And instantly the room goes deadly quiet, everyone is listening closely. You blunder on nervously in a voice that comes out as a very audible stage-whisper, 'What I mean is, that with all these people here –.' 'All these people' are now straining not to miss a single syllable.

'Aren't you pleased?' asks Janice in a normal voice.

'Of course I am pleased,' you answer, gazing round the company defensively, and then continue, 'it's just that – well I –,' and now you are so hopelessly confused that you don't really know what you want to say, so you kiss her and everyone in the room cheers loudly, then returns to their amusements.

A few moments pass during which you and Janice say nothing to each other and then you hear a girl's voice speaking above the tumult of the ludo game, TV and dinner conversation.

'Not like that Tommy, like this.' You look up and see that the fair-haired girl who had come up previously to speak to Janice, is now kneeling in front of one of the other children who has been trying to help her to remove the bandage from her knee.

'Sorry,' says Tommy 'is it alright now?'

Slowly the girl peels off the rest of the bandage and remarks that it will get better if the air is let in at it. Tommy agrees, adding shyly that if it will help, he will kiss it better. The girl laughs, and so he does. He kisses it once quickly, and then again more slowly. And at this point you see the girl place her hands gently on Tommy's head and begin stroking his hair. And now it seems her caresses are imperceptibly guiding him, for gradully he moves from kissing her knee to kissing her thigh as she pulls him closer to her. She is opening her legs and gently directing him to where she wishes him to kiss her.

You are so surprised, that all this happens before you believe it is happening and can do anything about it. The girl, realising that you are watching her, is looking very deeply at you. For the first time, you see that she is a full-grown woman and already, even as you watch, is becoming middle-aged and growing older with every moment.

'Stop, stop!' you cry out, half-rising from your seat to go towards her. Her hands are trembling now and yet you can see that she is holding even more tightly onto Tommy's hair, her face is lined and her fair hair has become white and very thin.

You are concious now that as you move towards her the room is growing darker and darker. You are so close that you can almost touch her, but it has grown so dark that you can hardly see her. You feel certain that if you take her in your arms she will grow no older, but, as you reach for her, she whispers fiercely, 'Stay away, stay away.'

Then gradually the light comes back, but where she is is still intense darkness. Then lastly, even there, light is restored. The fair-haired girl claps her hands merrily as if to chase away the last scraps of darkness. She gets to her feet and pulls Tommy to his then, without looking at all in your direction, she rejoins the ludo players.

You look round the room but no-one, it seems, has been paying the slightest attention to what has happened – people are still watching TV and eating and talking to each other. You are hoping that the elderly couple, at least, might acknowledge what has been happening, but they have started tickling each other now and aren't paying heed to anyone or anything else at all.

Only Janice is looking at you; it is as if she is asking you for an explanation when all the while you want an explanation from her. Even as you turn towards her the room is becoming larger and larger, and the closer you approach her, the further she seems to be in the distance. The light in the room is growing brighter and brighter until you can hardly see and your eyes hurt.

I have finished telling you that story now, but it seems to have disturbed you. You have woken up Janice. She asks why you're crying because of course your eyes are still running due to the intense light, and they still hurt. Tell her that there's nothing wrong. Tell her that you had a bad dream, a very bad dream: you were both in a room which kept getting larger and larger and so you were being forced further and further apart even as you were reaching for each other. And now she is kissing you and comforting you. You have made her happy. I'd like to tell you another bedtime story which I think I will call, 'The Tilting Room'. It's a funny title, isn't it?

Well, the story is about a room that is just full of odd crevices and corners, everything in it leans this way and that, and even the walls and ceilings don't quite meet at right angles! So close your eyes and relax for this is quite a long story. You no longer need be afraid of those gaps in eternity, those vast stretches of dead time, for you are in her arms and she is asleep. I will tell you a story that began long before you met her.

It starts: 'This room is really known only to you and me.' And even as I say these first words, I can feel the room tilting once more towards the earth's centre and towards the stars.

Conversations with Sheila

So many of memories. Like this. Listening to you. So many conversations. Like this. All like this. And afterwards? – afterwards there will be silence, as always. So many kinds of silence. But not yet. Please.

Are we sitting close? Touching, almost? Is your hair long? Your finger-nails painted?

– What was it Sheila said to me?

'Usually I wear my hair up, do you like that?'

And I said, 'Let it down, now. Just for me.'

'Would that please you?'

'Yes.'

'Then I shall, just for you.' She placed the phone on her lap while I waited, listening she picked the receiver up again – 'I'm shaking it out now. Its lying on my shoulders, on my back.'

Yes that was it. What we said. Her long black hair. I want to phone her. Now.

They say that this is a good place to live. I say that a place depends on the people who live there. The corridors are tidy and clean. No cigarette-packets on the floor, no spray-paint on the walls. And we've no doorman or cleaners – just good manners. The rich need looked-after, the poor need looked-after – but the middle-classes can look-after themselves. But really, I'm no snob. I wouldn't care where I lived so long as there were people nearby, any kind of people.

Or a telephone. If anyone asked what the greatest invention was I'd say the telephone. It was the first invention that was truly magic. It broke the laws of nature, everything else just extends them: you travel faster, see further, do things easier and so forth. But with a telephone I can talk with someone who is five thousand miles away. Not just send them a message, but actually converse with them. Not that I phone that distance everyday, or ever in fact; but whenever I pick up the phone I get a thrill to think how far away we are and yet I can hear their breathing so very close to me, almost as if they were whispering into my ear.

The first time I spoke with Sheila – I was trying to dial the operator and got her instead – the sound of her voice made me tremble so much that I could hardly say anything. She kept asking me who I was and what did I want? My mouth had gone dry.

'Ian,' I managed to say. 'My name is Ian.'

'And what do you want...Ian?'

What did I want? What do you give the man who has nothing? I told her I had enough money to live on, a pleasant flat and nothing else. She replied that I'd missed out something – a lovely voice.

I became very embarrassed and couldn't reply at first. Then I thanked her.

'Are you very unhappy?' she asked.

'No...that is, yes. I am.'

'I wish I was there to comfort you,' she said. Though I didn't really believe her, I agreed with her. And there was something that tempted me, something in her voice.

There are many kinds of silences and each of them is always the same length. Believe me. And she waited. She waited for me to ask her.

'If you were here, how would you comfort me?' There was another silence.

'I would take you in my arms,' she said. 'I would stroke your hair and kiss you.' That was what she said, 'I would take you in my arms. I would stroke your hair and kiss you.'

We often phone each other now. We have never met. We say what we would like to do to each other. Kiss you. Touch you. Undress you. Then once I tried to tell her that afterwards – afterwards? she asked warmly. That afterwards, I began again, I often, that is I almost always – another silence. Then she said, so do I.

'What do you do?' she asked and her voice seemed close, so very close to me – inside me. I described everything I did, and so did she.

Sheila and I. Her voice and mine. I would say anything for her. Do anything. The first time I told her I loved her she said nothing. I waited and waited. There was silence while she asked.

'What do lovers do together?'

'They make love.'

'Then let's make love together now. I am unbuttoning my blouse and my hand is caressing my breast. Take your tie off Ian, and undo your shirt. And tell me what it is you are doing.'

We often make love together now. We have never met. We say what we are doing to ourselves. Sometimes Sheila says what I must do and I say what she must do. Sometimes we are very, very close. Especially when we say we love each other.

I will phone her in a few minutes but there is so much to remember. The sound of her voice. The words she said. Laughter. Sighs. The silences to be remembered. So many kinds of silences. Of memories. Listening to her voice. So many conversations. Like this. All like this. And afterwards – afterwards there will be silence, as always.

I look at women sometimes. I've never met her and yet perhaps we have met without knowing. Sometimes I think I recognise her. I am looking at a woman who is sitting in a cafe, for example. I go in to buy cigarettes and there, at one of the tables, I see her. I hear her speaking close to me, inside me.

I try to catch her eye. So strongly, so longingly I want to sit with her. Touching. To buy her coffee, to be there with her. To spend the afternoon with her. We might stay chatting for a while and then maybe go for a walk together.

But she looks away. Always. I am so certain it is her that several times I have gone up to someone and asked if her name is Sheila. I don't do that now.

I answer when she calls me. Always. We can talk without being overheard. We are alone and I do whatever she says. Everything she says.

– And afterwards? Afterwards the clock will be ticking loudly and, outside, the rush-hour traffic will have begun. Another conversation will be over. I will have nothing more to say and, anyway, there will be no-one to hear me.

Perhaps if she walked into my flat and saw me sitting here smoking a cigarette and doing nothing – what might she think of me?

She would look round and see the fastidiousness with which I order my possessions; she would observe the neatness and the deliberation. Probably she would suspect me of being a cautious man, a passionless man, a lonely man with no sense for the spontaneous, the anarchic. She would condemn me to her silent pity.

Could she not guess that only in our conversations do I truly sense the men and women our intimacy excludes? – For they become inflexions in the voice that declares our love. And could she not realise that I myself, this room, and all the inhabitants and buildings of the city are indistinguishable from the silence that comes afterwards?

I have taken off my jacket. Sheila? Tell me what to do. What was it you said once? 'I would take you in my arms; I would stroke your hair and kiss you.' I can hear you saying it now.

The Child and The Man

When I was fourteen I fell in love for the last time. And then one night I was awakened by the sound of tapping on my window. Thinking it was the wind I turned over and tried to get back to sleep; but how quiet everything was – no rattling of slates nor roaring in the chimney, just this tap-tap on the window-pane. After several minutes of complete wakefulness I got out of bed. The tapping became more insistent as I went over to the curtains. I hoped to see my mother when I opened them – that is, I hoped to see the spirit of my mother, for she had been dead for fourteen years.

I had been brought up by my aunt Vera, a woman in her late forties, both my parents having been killed in a car-crash shortly after I was born. She was my mother's sister, and as degenerate a woman as I am ever likely to meet. Is her kind dying out now? I sincerely hope so, if there is to be any hope for my generation. My earliest memories are of her thick fingers prodding my stomach to assure herself that I was growing fat. She had a horror of thinness and was herself a remarkably stout woman.

When I was five years old, each evening I would dutifully get up from my toys when it was time to go to bed, then get changed into my pyjamas by myself and under her direction. She insisted that I was never to be completely naked but do the top half first and then the bottom half. Gradually I accustomed myself to the method and speed of undress she wished. Sometimes she would say, 'Not so fast Paul, careful now, you might tear that shirt,' meanwhile her finger-nail would impatiently scratch the side of the arm-chair until I had adjusted to the desired rate. Soon the whole operation could be performed in complete silence but for the scratching of her finger-nail to slow down my actions, and let her linger over any detail that particularly appealed to her that evening. To speed up any part that seemed to cause her momentary impatience, she repeatedly slapped the chair-arm with the palm of her hand, gradually slowing down until my process of undress arrived at the next detail she wished to study, any finer adjustments then being made by her finger-nail. And all the while with her free hand she conveyed marshmallows to her mouth and chewed noiselessly, and gazed at me. If she wanted me to turn round she would give me a marshmallow.

We lived in a basement, and my aunt, when she wasn't eating marshmallows, would often smoke woodbines. She warned me not to smoke for then I would never grow big and tall like my father, but sometimes I used to go into the garden and smoke until I was nearly sick. I also used to smoke in the bathroom, leaving the window open. I frequently wondered what my father had looked like and so I would wet my hair and part it as he had in his photographs. Then, with a cigarette in my mouth, I would look at myself in the mirror. If my aunt came knocking at the door asking what I was doing in there all day, I would quickly re-comb my hair, put out the cigarette, put my father's photo up my jumper, and having made sure all the smoke had cleared, I would flush the toilet and leave.

When I came out she would often ask me if I had been 'up to anything'. I'd reply that I didn't know what she meant, and then she'd say that I wasn't normal. Usually though she would just pat me on the stomach, saying that at least I wasn't thin and that was a blessing. One day, however, I risked taking in the whole family album which had some photographs of my mum and dad together with me, taken when I was very small. I spent ages trying my dad's various partings and expressions, and even some of my mum's smiles and ways of tilting her head. When I came out my aunt asked if I'd been looking at pictures. My expression must have given me away immediately, because she said 'Aha!'

That evening while I was going through the customary ritual of getting ready for bed, although I was almost ten years old by this time, she asked me if I liked looking at pictures. I didn't say anything. Then she asked me if I'd ever seen 'the real thing' or just pictures. I answered that of course I had, but I couldn't remember anything as I was very young at the time. To this she smiled with lascivious pleasure and remarked that I was a smart one. Then she asked if I would like to see the real thing, but added that I would not see everything, not just yet anyway. At this I broke out in a big smile. I was very happy because I thought she meant that somehow I was going to see my mum and dad and that I had misunderstood what being dead meant, for really they were just away somewhere for a while and waiting for me to grow up from being a small boy.

When she noticed how excited I was, her face became flushed and she said that I really was a smart one and no mistake. Then she unbuttoned her blouse and exposed her very large breasts. I was rather puzzled by this turn of affairs and was uncertain what was happening. 'Don't be afraid,' she said, 'it's alright seeing that I'm not your mother or sister. Look at them, they're real, not pictures.' I felt cheated as this was not at all what I'd expected; I wanted to see my mum and dad. Then she asked me if I wanted to touch them. I didn't want to touch them, and said so. She kept on asking if I wanted to, saying how soft they were and so nice to touch. Finally she grabbed my hand, and they did feel nice to touch. She said again that I was a smart one and I should soon grow up big and tall like my father, – then I burst into tears. She comforted me and sent me to bed with my mouth full of marshmallows.

As can be imagined, things did not stop there, and over the next few months she introduced me to many kinds of intimacies. She began taking me to her bed sometimes where I would have to lie close beside her in the darkness. Then one night she said I wasn't to be afraid but she was going to make me grow big and tall like my father. I became afraid. But soon I felt a strange thrilling and shivering sensation run all over me for the first time – and this I took to be the spirit of my father being raised within me.

As I said, when I was fourteen I fell in love for the last time and, considering the way aunt Vera brought me up, it's nothing short of miraculous that I fell in love at all. She used the word 'love' when ever we were in bed together saying, 'You do love me

John, don't you? (John was my father's name) – to which I had
to reply, 'Yes Vera, I love you.' The first time that this happened,
along with my father's spirit being raised, proved too much for
me: I went to the bathroom afterwards and cried and tried to
smoke a woodbine; then I went to my own bed even though I
knew it would be cold. Soon however I stopped crying
afterwards and would smoke my woodbine in bed beside her –
she liked that, though it was the only time she ever let me smoke.

She always made me go and sleep in my own bed afterwards.
At first, as I said, I really wanted to get away from her as soon as
possible, but as it was always so cold by myself I asked her once if
I couldn't stay and sleep with her instead. At this she became
quite angry, and as she was seldom even cross with me really, I
never asked her again. What she wanted me to do it seemed, was
to smoke my woodbine then, without saying goodnight or
anything, just slip out of her bed and go through to my own. The
only exception to this was on the night of my fourteenth
birthday. I had had some friends round for tea and when they'd
gone she got very drunk. After I left her bed she came through to
my room and climbed in beside me, then she put her arms tightly
about me and immediately fell fast asleep. She snored so loudly
that I'm sure I didn't sleep all night but lay there trapped. In the
morning when she woke up she just looked at me, bit her lip and
said, 'Oh Paul!' Then she got up and rushed through to her own
room; later I heard her crying. That was the only time we really
slept together, though, as I said, I did very little sleeping.

For a short time after that she did not take me to her bed to do
'real things', as she called them, as often as before; but when she
did she was in a real frenzy, demanding that I tell her how much
John loved her, and then that I prove it 'to her complete
satisfaction' as she would say. It was at this time that I started
going out with Margaret, a girl at my school. Though I had seen
her every day for years one day I seemed to see her for the first
time. I felt as if she was all around me and within me. At last I
summoned up enough courage to ask a friend of mine to ask a
friend of hers to ask her if she fancied me at all. And in no time we
were skipping school together to sit all afternoon in cafes or

cinemas holding hands. We didn't say we were in love, of course, in fact we didn't say very much at all; just held hands and squeezed them occasionally depending upon what record was playing or what the hero and heroine were saying or doing.

I was afraid of my aunt finding out about Margaret. Somehow I thought it would be better if she did not know. Life continued at home very much as it always done: she took me to her bed about once a fortnight and, excepting that, I suppose things were perfectly normal. But once I started going out with Margaret I dreaded my aunt's caresses and endearments.

Then one night she wanted me to come to her and I wouldn't. I didn't say anything but just lay there in my bed very, very tense. She pleaded with me, shouted at me and eventually she slapped me across the face before stalking back to her room. When she'd gone I relaxed and started drifting back into dreams about Margaret where we kissed lingeringly and spoke tender words to each other over and over again. I was falling asleep when the door opened once more and in walked Aunt Vera. I was ready to scream to her to get out, to leave me alone, when she said she'd come to apologise. After a moment I replied that it was alright, and then she remarked that it was time we had a serious talk. I didn't know what she wanted to talk about, but I was afraid that somehow she had found out about Margaret and wanted me to stop seeing her.

She sat on the edge of my bed and began talking to me about schoolwork and what kinds of jobs I might get when I left. As she didn't seem to be going to say anything about Margaret and as I was very tired anyway, I started falling asleep and so lost much of what she was saying until I became aware of her voice calling, 'John, John,' softly but firmly. Before I realised what was happening, she had begun to raise the spirit of my father. Again I felt that delicious thrill run over my body, and I reached for and pulled her in beside me saying, 'John loves you, John loves you.' Afterwards when I had finished my woodbine and aunt Vera had gone back to her room, I thought about Margaret. I fell asleep trying to picture her as she had looked that day sitting next to the window in class.

Lately I had noticed that I was growing more and more to resemble my father as he looked in some of the photographs. Did this mean, I wondered, that his spirit was growing stronger and stronger within me? Did it mean that when I had grown to resemble him completely, his spirit would completely take over and I would no longer exist? Then quite suddenly I understood everything: I was the child and he was the man; and now that the child was growing up the man was taking over. When aunt Vera raised his spirit within me for the first time she said that I was not to be afraid; but his spirit frightened me, and each time since it seemed stronger and stronger. People sometimes said, 'he's only a child', and now I understood what they meant. I thrilled every time my father's spirit was raised within me. I was exhilarated and frightened at the same time. For a few moments I sensed what it was to be a man, and at the same time I sensed my own death.

Then one night I heard that gentle tapping on my window and I knew my mother had come to see my father, whose spirit her presence would further strengthen within me. I opened the curtains expecting to see her as in the photographs, but I saw nothing, just an empty street. My aunt must have heard me walking about for she came into the room at that moment and asked if anything was the matter. I told her that I had just been closing the window which had woken me by its rattling. This seemed to work for she said goodnight and went back to her room.

I lay in bed listening to hear if the tapping would start again. Several times I even got out of bed and went over to the window to check that there was no-one there. By this time I was too disturbed to sleep and lay there wide-awake. My father's spirit had been raised and he was angry. Then he began to speak to me for the first time. Why hadn't I gone to the window quicker? Didn't I want to see my mother? Didn't I care about her? I was too afraid to reply. I lay there in the darkness without moving while his voice continued, shouting inside me. Eventually he calmed down. I told him that I was very tired. I did not tell him that I had missed him all these years and that now I was terrified of him.

He said that we had much to talk about having been apart for so long, so I told him all I had done as far back as I could remember. I told him about my aunt and the evening rituals, the marshmallows – which he thought very amusing, about the photographs, and how my aunt showed me what was 'real', and how at those times I had felt his spirit rise within me. And he said that that was good, but now we could talk together at any time of the day or night, I wasn't to go to aunt Vera unless he said so.

Then he told me about my mother and what the family had done together when I was just a baby. He told me where we'd been when the photographs I knew so well had been taken. He then went on to describe how he had met my mother when he had been doing his National Service, and that was why in some of the photographs he was dressed as a soldier. When I asked him what it was like being in the army, he began telling me the most fantastic stories of tanks and battles, and gradually I fell asleep.

Next day as I was on my way to school he began speaking to me again. He was asking about Margaret and I told him that he would see her soon in class, and also that I was going a walk with her at lunchtime. He kept asking about her. I had to tell him how I first met her, what she looked like, what she was wearing, had I ever seen her naked? He made me angry and I shouted to him to shut up, but he just laughed. I tried to explain to him that with Margaret it was different because I wanted to be able to fall properly in love with her, not just do with her the things I had to do with my aunt.

All through the morning lessons he kept on at me. He wouldn't let me concentrate on my work. Didn't I want to see her naked? Didn't I want to touch her? He just would not shut up. Did I know the facts of life? he asked me. I tried to ignore him. Then he began telling me that many women are almost as different physically from each other as they are from men. Just as they have different kinds and colours of hair, so they have different kinds of bodies under their clothes. I could not help looking round the class at some of the girls and I felt his spirit getting restless inside me. That's what people mean, he continued, when they say they suit each other. You don't know if you and Margaret suit each other yet, do you? That's the danger about falling in love, he remarked after a short pause, especially for the first time, that if people find out too late that they don't suit each other, then sometimes they are so unhappy that they kill themselves.

Even though I'd heard people talk like that, especially in the films or on TV, I felt he was trying to trick me into doing something that he wanted to do and I didn't. He wanted me to do with Margaret all the things I did with Aunt Vera so that his spirit would grow stronger and stronger, and eventually take control completely and I would no longer exist. He said that he was warning me about falling in love, for, if she and I didn't suit each other, then perhaps I might kill myself, and he and I would be parted again, this time forever. Maybe he was telling the truth but I wasn't sure. I knew that he and I would part soon because I could not remain both a man and a child for long. What I hoped was that if Margaret loved me then together our love might be strong enough to resist him. Even though I doubted there being any truth in the matter, I began to worry whether we did suit each other or not.

I met Margaret at lunchtime and suggested we went for our walk down by the river. As we left the school she began to tell me what had happened at her home the previous night, and what she had seen on television. Then she asked me if a boy in the class called Steve fancied Helen, a friend of hers. She was in the middle of chattering about this when we turned off the street to go down to the river. I interrupted her to say that I loved her. I took her in my arms and looked deep into her eyes as I had seen them do in the pictures. When she didn't reply I kissed her softly on the forehead and said that I hoped she loved me. She blushed and squeezed my hand, but said nothing.

I smiled, but inside I was frantic. Why didn't she just answer a simple yes or no like in the films? So I asked her again. This time she replied that we were really going steady, weren't we? Then she paused for a moment and added that, yes, she thought she was in love with me but she wasn't sure yet; she would have to think about it, and would let me know after school. When she said this, my father told me that I would have to find out if we suited each other. I would have to find out now, he urged, before it was too late.

We walked further down the river, onto a long stretch where the path was hidden from the road by a line of trees. Margaret started asking me about Steve again, and I said that I'd no idea if he fancied Helen or even if he fancied anyone at all. I tried to speak normally but a fierce dialogue was raging inside me between my father and myself. At length I interrupted her again to ask her if she thought we would suit each other. She kissed me, then said that she thought we would. We kissed again for a long time, and didn't say anything.

Make certain, before it's too late, my father broke in fiercely. I felt certain that he was setting a trap for me. I wanted to resist him. He began to bully me saying, touch her breast, that will relax her. Caress it gently, he whispered. You must. You must find out if you suit each other. You're lying, I said to him, you're trying to trick me. But he ignored me. Let your hand slide gently from her breast, he urged, move it gradually down her jersey and try to put it up her skirt.

She wouldn't let me do that , however, and began pushing my hand away. But she has not stopped kissing you, he said. You can try again. She pushed my hand away. You can try once more. Then she began kissing me very hard, she was letting my hand slide up her thighs. I became afraid because I felt his spirit was growing stronger within me. She pushed me away again. His spirit was growing stronger and stronger and I had to try again, and again she pushed me away – this time, however, she stopped kissing me as well. I was not going to try any more no matter what he said, for I could feel him raised very strong within me and he was tense.

Again she pushed me away very firmly, saying that perhaps we should be getting back to school. I told her that I was sorry, but I had just wanted to know for certain that we suited each other. She said that it was alright really and, though she was sure that we did suit each other, she didn't want to rush things. Now, he said, now.

And already I was watching him, whose spirit now filled my whole body so that it was tingling and stinging, use my hands to force her legs apart and rip off the tights she would not let me place my fingertips inside. I watched in horror as Margaret's face was pushed backwards by my hand and held to the ground by my fingers gripping her hair. I tried to speak to her to tell her not to be afraid, not to struggle or I was sure my father would kill her so strong did he feel within me. I wanted to avert my eyes, to stop my ears but he would not let me, saying that I had to listen and I had to look to make certain the she and I suited each other. When he was at his fullest strength my whole body shook and thrilled – and then he was gone.

Margaret lay on the ground in tears. Her face was smeared with dirt and blood but that did not matter because I loved her. When I told her that I loved her, she tried to stand up; she seemed very weak so I held onto her in case she fell. Then she said I was never to touch her again or to speak to her again. I watched helplessly as she stumbled off along the bank. Then my father began speaking to me again. She has refused your love and you will be very unhappy, but do not worry because I will be with you, he said. He was trying to sound comforting but I knew he was exulting. Now that Margaret would have nothing to do with me he thought that my love for her was of no consequence – that I would soon kill myself and so give way to him completely.

'But I love you,' I cried after her as she staggered towards the end of the line of trees. 'I love you, I don't want to hurt you.' She said nothing. Then she stumbled, and I ran towards her to help her all the while crying that I loved her. I was in tears now and desperate; inside me my father's spirit was laughing. I caught up with her and she tried to shake me off, but she was too weak.

Then my father became serious: this is not the woman you love, he said. 'Yes she is, she is,' I stammered. She was staring at my face and looking far into the distance; she was very frightened. The tears were streaming down my cheeks as I held her, my hands on her shoulders. 'I love you, can't you understand?' I pleaded.

Then my father began gripping her shoulders more tightly in my hands. He must have been very strong because he lifted her up off her feet and threw her onto the ground. This is not the woman you love, he said, look at her. And though her face was all dirt and blood I said yes it is, this is Margaret whom I love. Then he picked up a stone in my hand and struck her face with it, and still I said I recognise her because I love her so deeply. Again and again he struck her until at last I could no longer recognise her, then he stopped. Do you know who she is? he asked. No, I answered. Come with me, he said.

We went home. The house was empty. My aunt was out. I spread the family photographs out on the table. There is my mother. But I can't recognise her. She was killed in a car-crash. I know that I am dying as well. I am her child. The spirit of the man she loved is growing stronger and killing me. He killed Margaret the girl that I love. He was driving the car when my mother was killed. He ran it into a wall killing her like this and like this and like this – my finger-nail scratches across her photograph. I am looking at the photograph now, it is torn – and all at once I do recognise my mother. I saw her today in fact, when I was returning from a walk by the river. She was lying on the bank.

I keep hearing myself differently, my voice is changing all the time – it is my father's voice speaking more and more. He is saying Aunt Vera will be coming home soon and I must put away the photographs. I must not tell her about recognising my mother today – that is to be a secret. I must not tell her about Margaret who does not want me to touch her or to speak to her again.

I saw my mother today and I stood beside her while she was asleep. I wondered what she was dreaming about. Tonight she will come to me in secret; she will tap on the window-pane; she will take me away to be with her for always. My aunt will know nothing of this.

My aunt is here. My father's voice is speaking to her, and he will always speak to her from now on. My voice is a whisper that only my mother will hear. He is joking with her and I can hardly hear what he is saying. She is laughing. I can see her teeth and her tongue. She is patting my stomach and I cannot hear what she is saying. His spirit is everywhere as my fingers undo the buttons on her blouse; he is laughing. Knowing that my mother is coming for me I am no longer afraid.

Now she is breathing awkwardly, quickly. Her eyes stare into the distance. I want to approach where my father is now; I want to feel what he is touching now with my hands. Everything is different to him. He is telling her that it is different, he is telling how it is different. She is getting more excited than she has ever been before. Now he is telling her that he loves her; at last he is speaking for himself, at last he is saying that he loves her and has always loved her.

She is pulling him closer and closer. She whispers hoarsely and excitedly into his ear, 'Who loves me, tell me who loves me?' Then I hear him reply, 'Paul loves you, Vera, Paul loves you.'

Complete Strangers

Suddenly I remember that it is still the afternoon and if I go now I might manage a few more calls before five o'clock. All I need to do, of course, is get up, put on my clothes, collect my sample case and leave. I needn't say anything except goodbye. The woman won't care – after all we are still complete strangers. And even if she does, what will that matter once the front door has closed after me and I am driving away in my car? I begin to get up.

The woman, thinking that I am moving just to make myself more comfortable, gives me a hug and kisses me on the forehead. I return the kiss and settle down beside her again. Sometimes I can't decide whether I am very polite of very cowardly.

The bedroom is a modern bedroom. I was in an identical one two weeks ago: the same suite, the same matching curtains – but the woman was slimmer and had red hair. Their tastes in art differ however; last fortnight's had a photograph of her husband stuck into the corner of a Van Gogh above the bed. Today's has a photograph of her dog stuck into the corner of a Van Gogh above the bed. I prefer dogs to husbands, though as conversation pieces husbands are better–

'– I'll have to throw you out soon. Kids'll be coming back.' She kissed me.

Good on them, I think to myself as I get up. I dress quickly. The woman, she's called Hilda, puts on a dressing-gown and we kiss goodbye in the hall.

'You don't mind me not coming out to say goodbye?' she asks anxiously.

I hesitate for just the right length of time before replying, 'Of course not.'

The woman smiles. I smile back. With mock gallantry I raise and kiss her hand. My timing perfect, I become sincere.

'I'll phone you,' I say seriously, nodding as if in emphasis – I give her hand a parting squeeze, let it go slowly as though reluctantly, and then leave.

I am a good salesman and, at twenty-four, definitely one of the most promising in the company. Whenever I am asked for my 'secret' I give the same reply:

'Don't sell the product, sell yourself. If they'll buy *you*, they'll buy what you're selling. They'll trust you – or, better still, she'll trust you. That's why it's easier to sell to a woman than to a man – not because they're more gullible, which they're not, but because they're more trusting.

'My "secret" is that I'm good at making people trust me. By good I mean quick.'

After driving round the estate and visiting a few more houses I decide it is time to call it a day and go home. Hilda had quite long nails – I hope she has not left any scratch-marks on my back.

Four hours later I have had dinner and am sitting watching TV. My wife Susan is sitting beside me. The room would be in darkness but for the glare from the screen. Susan is sitting close to me. Her hand is on my knee.

If I don't put my arm round her in the next few minutes she will feel hurt. I do not want to hurt her; I do not want to put my arm around her. I keep looking at the TV.

A quiz show is reaching its climax with the audience becoming hysterical and shouting out advice to the remaining contestants – a man and a woman. The man is grinning uncontrollably and keeps looking in every direction; the woman doesn't even smile. The compere is waving a very bright orange envelope above the heads of the lucky couple. In her excitement Susan grips my knee. I tense.

'Sorry love,' she says, turning for a moment to give me a quick kiss on the cheek.

I glance at her. She is staring straight ahead, her face and body lit by colours from the screen. Without taking her eyes from the TV she has a drink from the glass beside her. Her hand begins to stroke my thigh. I do nothing. The compere is about to open the envelope. Susan's hand has moved to my inside-leg.

'What do you think it is?' she asks suddenly.

'Pardon?'

'The rate of flow of the Mississippi. What do you think? Imagine getting a dream-holiday just for that.' Her hand is rubbing me gently now, but more firmly. She is still staring straight ahead.

The contestants stand side by side facing the audience – the man seems to keep changing colour, the woman looks quite pale. The compere is genial and bullying at the same time. The audience ignores any pleas he makes for silence.

I can feel my fly being unzipped and all at once I am very tired – couldn't she just let me be? I feel a yawn beginning in my stomach then rising to my chest. By changing my position slightly and putting my arm around Susan so she rests her head on my shoulder, I manage to yawn unobtrusively.

'– about seven million, two hundred thousand cubic feet per second,' I remark casually.

'– What?' Susan's hand stops for a moment.

'The rate of flow of the Mississippi; seven million, two–'

'– Oh yes, of course,' says Susan with a laugh as she begins stroking again. She can feel a response now and presses herself closer to me.

An hour later I am dozing in front of the fire. On TV a man with a red bow tie is explaining why the Keynsian attitude to public expenditure is not only outmoded, but arguably counter-productive in a stagflation situation. He is grey haired and lively; he is enthusiastic about his multi-coloured graphs.

Susan lies stretched out on the couch, she looks asleep. Seen by the light from the screen her hair is grey-green, and her skin and blouse have a bright bluish overlay – but only for a moment. As the picture changes so does Susan. I watch her appearance alter every few seconds: she becomes harsh, then yielding, mutilated then innocent. Taking care not to waken her I lean over and kiss her.

A few minutes afterwards I turn off the TV. Susan stirs restlessly. I cross the room and switch on the main light.

'Sorry, I must have dozed off,' mumbles Susan still half-asleep. 'What time is it?'

'After eleven. Time for bed,' I reply and start to collect the glasses.

'Oh, leave them,' she says, 'I'll do it all tomorrow. Come and sit here for a moment.' She makes a space for me on the couch.

'You must be very tired, love, all that selling and then ... you know,' she continues with a smile indicating the rug. I manage to smile back.

'Yes, I'm pretty beat,' I agree as I sit down beside her taking her hand in mine. I look at her and, with mock gallantry kiss it. Then I turn it inwards and kiss the soft palm. I remain like this: her hand held to my lips for several moments. But held tightly. Though I do not want to cause her pain, I cannot let go. I grip harder.

Suddenly I know I am about to burst into tears. Must I crush every bone in her hand before she will comfort me?

Susan has caught her breath at the sudden pain. She jerks her hand free.

'–Sorry, love,' I say quickly, 'I don't know my own strength.'

'I'm glad you do usually,' Susan replies massaging her fingers. Then she holds them up. 'Kiss them better?'

I do so gently, contritely. Susan leans closer as though about to take me in her arms.

I stand up and say lightly, 'Time for bed,' then take her hand again. 'I've got lots of hard selling to do tomorrow to keep you in the style to which you have become accustomed.' I indicate the room with a broad sweep of my arm.

Laughing, Susan allows herself to be pulled to her feet. For a moment we stand still in each other's arms and kiss. I give her a hug then slowly release her.

A Few Days with William

I no longer need to look into the mirror to see him. His name is William. He is standing at the bar with a pint and a packet of cigarettes to hand. He isn't waiting for anyone, he doesn't need to. He is accepted. He has been working hard all day and now he is resting at the bar.

William lights a cigarette and glances over the tables to see who's in tonight. A few familiar faces, a few strangers. Where has he seen her before? A shop perhaps? in the street? She recognises him, her eyes meet his. Sandra isn't it? I'm William, I thought we'd met before, I wouldn't forget your smile, no seriously. She laughs. I'm an architect, usually look in here on the way home for dinner, he says. Nothing fancy you understand but if you'd care to ...

William is walking home. He is wearing a smart new coat. He will cook dinner for Sandra who is walking beside him. He is telling her about some of his clients and making her laugh. She has a lovely smile. She is walking beside him.

'Cold enough for a half-bottle' William says, and the man laughs as he wraps it up. Outside again with Sandra. William is singing for her as they walk along the road. This is the place.

The sound of the key in the latch. Shutting the door behind him and locking it, he looks to see if there are any letters then walks through to the kitchen and turns on the T.V. There is nothing to eat except Corn Flakes and a tin of sardines so he has some then pours himself a mug of whisky. On T.V. he watches a documentary about somewhere in Africa followed by the news and then a programme about penguins, after which he goes to bed and finishes the whisky there.

Sandra is lying beside him in the darkness. She says that she is glad he recognised her in the pub. She thought she knew him but wasn't sure. William kisses her. William puts his arm round her and pulls her close.

Because he has drunk a half-bottle of whisky he sometimes forgets Sandra is there. He keeps forgetting and lies there in the darkness alone and drunk. Then he remembers her again and makes love to her until she is not there anymore.

What if the pavement does slide? the walls relax? and the roads unwind? Then he will walk trailing his new coat in the snow. The sky curves down and the road curves, and the trees and the hills all curve – towards him; but William can cope. He's walking on the earth like a dog on a ball, it's spinning and he's keeping his feet – everything's curving round him. And perhaps it's time to sit on his new coat, on the snow, on the earth.

A man, a woman and a dog. William is carrying his new coat until they're past and now he can trail it if he wants. William is keeping his feet while the earth spins. He's performing and nobody's watching.

His name is William. His wife has red hair and lives in Manchester. She is not worth talking about. William knows the score and doesn't want to get caught again. William plays the field. He is resting up now for a few weeks. He's still got the old magic and can wave his wand whenever he wants! This evening he is at a party. He's standing by the mantlepiece, off-duty as it were, giving some of the others a chance. Wives and husbands mostly – William's well out of that. Every so often he has a quick dip into the typing pool. A few strokes and out again. Maybe a paddle just now, in and out – people expect it. See who's here. A few familiar faces, a few strangers. And there's one: dewy-eyed, firm tits, long hair and boots. Looks a bit pissed. Now for the charm, William, the old magic.

'And what's your name darling?'

'Piss off William.'

'That's a funny name darling.'

Everyone's looking at William. The floor keeps tilting and William keeps sliding against the sofa. A lot of people are talking to him, suddenly too many.

Suddenly it's bitterly cold and quiet. William can keep his balance now and no-one's looking. She smiled at him, a lovely smile. Can I get you a drink? Lovely long hair you have. And, if you don't mind my saying it, such lovely firm breasts. William is putting his arm round her and she is turning to kiss him. Her name is Ann, perhaps. William is walking home with her, with Ann; she is wearing a denim skirt. She is smiling at him. She has a lovely smile. William is falling in love.

The sound of the key in the latch. Get the light out William. Ann is here, she is getting in beside you. Remember her smile, her long hair.

William feels sick and Ann is lying on the ceiling beckoning him towards her. The ceiling tilts and William can feel Ann's finger-tips pressing on his eyes; her hair is unravelling in his mouth. He reaches for her and pulls her close to him until she disappears.

I have been observing William Coverdale for the last eight minutes. He has been sitting at his desk breaking pencils. It is his birthday. He seldom speaks now. He meets people's eyes only for a moment, for then their eyes catch fire. His mother once baked him a cake for his birthday. She lit the candles then he blew them out with one big breath. Everyone in the office is watching him. He is snapping the pencils one by one. Everyone in the office is waiting. There are only six pencils left.

William looks round the office and meets everyone's eyes for long enough that they become flame. The room is filled with candles so that when anyone moves the flames shake and the shadows scatter against the walls. William is a year older today, and the candles have been set in a circle round him. When he breaks the last pencil they will be blown out and everything will be in darkness.

William is about to speak, he needs more pencils hurry. Beyond the circle of candles William has seen the deepest darkness – and he knows that the candles will soon burn down.

When he blew them out with one big breath everyone cheered

and his mother switched the light back on. The candles looked dull and dirty then, with a thin trail of smoke that made his nose wrinkle. He is holding the last pencil in his hand. William is resisting the urge to break it. He is holding it between his fingers. Perhaps if he is strong enough he can hold everything just as it is at this moment.

But his hands know their work better than he, and William watches as his fingers snap the pencil neatly in half. Everything is in darkness and he is alone. The women he has known and with whom he has spent lifetimes – they are here, and everything is here. Out of this darkness he can now create whatever he loves and whatever loves him.

3

The Cousins

There were six trees in the garden. Colin stood at the upstairs window counting them while he fingered the spots on his forehead. Behind him his cousin Sally lay on the couch and was telling him how her friend Tibs and another girl had played with a glass tumbler and letters to spell out spirit-messages. Colin had two new spots this morning and had to keep touching them.

'Not anyone can do it,' Sally was saying. 'You have to be really psychic first and – ' she burst out laughing '– and Tibs got it wrong; she thought you had to be really sick first, and ate lots of chocolate and cream and then – '

Colin counted the trees again. This was his holidays – staying at his rotten uncle and aunt's, in the rotten hills, in the rotten Borders. His rotten uncle had gone fishing without him. His rotten aunt had gone shopping without her. One, two, three, four, five, six rotten trees in the rotten garden. And his spots were getting worse.

Phil said it was shaving that started them. Phil usually knew what he was talking about – but Colin only shaved once a week, and certainly never shaved his forehead.

'Me, Tibs and Fran did it twice. It's easy.' Sally sat up – it was uncomfortable being a merry widow, on this couch anyway. She was thirteen and growing. Sometimes when she woke up she was an old crone and would grip her fingers tightly into the air to claw her way out of bed; then, immediately her feet touched the floor, she would begin feeling all the confidence of a fully experienced young woman. She would walk about the room then open the window wide saying to herself 'experienced', saying it slowly, languidly. Several times she had tried saying it aloud but her voice sounded so thin she felt embarrassed.

'All you have to do is write out the letters A–Z on bits of paper with one for 'yes', one for 'no' and one with a holy cross. And then – ' realising her cousin hadn't interrupted her, she continued with more confidence, 'and then, we put all the letters in a circle on the top of a table, with 'yes' and 'no' opposite each other. It doesn't matter where the holy cross goes so long as it is in the circle. Then we put a glass tumbler in the centre, and wait.'

There were six, stiff straight trees in the garden. 'Wait?' Colin had only been half-listening to his cousin. Maybe if he didn't squeeze his spots at all, as the doctor had advised, there wouldn't be so many – but those that remained would look even worse, white-tipped and almost bursting. He touched his forehead again. The two new ones were already large and sore, he couldn't just ignore them – not ripening like that.

'Wait for what?' he asked as he turned away so his cousin couldn't see what he was doing.

'For the spirits, of course.'

'Think they'll come just because you stick a tumbler on a table – they're not wasps, are they?'

'– But there's the letters and everything,' Sally protested, then standing up she continued, 'and anyway you've got to call them – and put your finger on the glass. It's upside-down.'

'Of course, it's the tumbler's upside-down. *That's* how they get in,' Colin interrupted sarcastically while performing a mock-gesture, hand to his forehead, of sudden realisation. 'And how do you call them?'

Sally became serious, 'We say: is anybody there?'

At this her cousin made an exaggerated exploding noise as of suppressed laughter. 'Is anybody there?' he repeated. 'Is that all?'

Sally, although rather hurt by all this ridicule, continued, 'It's quite enough to say "Is anybody there?" – though it may need repeating.' She said this with such dignity that her cousin, forgetting to sneer, asked if there had been any response.

'Oh, yes,' replied Sally excitedly, 'each time I did it, that was twice,' she admitted 'it worked. The first time we got Tibs's great-great-hundreds-of-times-great-grandfather, and next time a woman who was Irish.'

'And what did they say?'

'Well, not a lot really. Tibs and Fran and me were so excited the glass kept slipping and we had to keep starting over again. The Irish woman was called Marie-Thérèse, and that took ages to spell-out because we started about a hundred times and we hadn't a hyphen; and then she left.'

'Maybe they're not allowed to stay for long.' Colin seemed interested now.

'Maybe. – And then Tibs's great-great-etc-grandfather took ages as if he couldn't spell, which wouldn't surprise me as Tibs can hardly spell either. But it worked. It did.' She looked to her cousin enthusiastically.

Colin had managed to stop counting the trees – and he relaxed. This was only the third day of his holidays. He would have much preferred sitting in the cafe at home, being bored. The cafe was boring, the town was boring, his friends were boring – they would talk about death and wonder if even that was as boring as sitting in the cafe. And so the days would pass.

But here, staying with his cousin, his spots were getting worse – and he was worried. Just before he left home Mike, who once claimed to have screwed his dog, told him that spots came from wanking. Anyone, he said, could tell at a glance who wanked and who didn't. 'You do,' he stated abruptly. Colin could not deny it. Not often though, not like Mike who boasted he sometimes did it eight times in a day; and his face was a mess, as if a thick and very seedy strawberry jam had been smeared over it. He didn't seem to care either.

For Colin, however, going into the classroom, even going downstairs to breakfast, could be torture if some new eruption had taken place during the night. There it was, poised on his forehead or pushing out from his cheek, red, soft and perhaps slightly leaking. It went into the room before him and he came after, almost as though he were hiding behind it. And now, according to Mike, everyone in the room – even his mother – would know what he did when he locked his bedroom door. He was horrified.

No more wanking – that was the only solution. But what about the spots that remained? Would they clear up by themselves? After three days he had begun wondering if he could wait. Another three days – nearly a week – and he was wondering if it was worth it, there seemed no difference. Maybe he should just settle for spots and masturbation, there seemed to be a certain tragic self-sufficiency to it.

Then he came here. He held out for a further two days, and last night had given way. After eight agitated days the wank had been good but brief – and, immediately, he had felt wretched and betrayed. So here he was, the morning-after, standing by the window with his guilt writ large for all the world to see, in a couple of lumpy shiners on his forehead – like a pair of horns.

There were six trees in the garden. He had felt himself stiffen as he stood there counting them over and over again. He kept touching his new spots, half-listening to Sally's talk about her seance. He had to stop counting the trees – but he was stiffening more and more. Each number from one to six seemed to tell differently and suggestively of pleasure within his grasp. He had to turn away from Sally. Back to the trees. Five, six, one, two three – how voluptuous these numbers were sounding, and he with his piece of timber, this seventh tree, growing at an alarming rate!

He had to stop counting. His cousin kept on about Tibs and her seance. Colin knew that some people had tried to receive spirit-messages at school, but nothing much had happened – maybe it would work here in an old farmhouse in the middle of nowhere. Whatever, thinking about it had stopped him counting the trees and he felt relaxed enough to turn round to Sally and say:

'OK. Let's try it. There's some writing-paper in that desk. I'll get the scissors from the kitchen, and a glass. Do you think this table will be alright?'

Sally's greater experience in psychic matters being thus acknowledged, she considered the small tea-table very gravely.

'It has three legs,' she pronounced.

'Does that matter?'

'I don't think so – but three is a magic number, I think.' Then after a pause as if she had been consulting some unseen familiar, she said, 'No – it will be all right.'

She tried it with her hands. 'It's quite strong and steady; also the top is shiny so the glass should slide easily enough – that's really quite important,' she added.

Colin was impressed. 'OK, Sally,' he said, 'I'll do A–M, the 'yes' and the 'no' – you do N–Z and the holy cross. What size?'

His cousin showed him how to make the letters, eight from each sheet of writing-paper. When they were ready Colin began laying them out on the table.

'*In* the way – so the spirits can read them, silly.' Colin did as he was told and in a few minutes the circle was completed when Sally placed the holy cross.

'Now?'

'The glass in the centre. Upside-down.' she said with emphasis. Dutifully her cousin placed the glass as directed, then he watched Sally put the tip of her first finger on the tumbler.

'Now you,' indicated Sally.

Colin hesitated.

'Come on,' she said.

'This one?'

'Yes,' answered Sally with a sigh of exaggerated patience.

As if he expected an electric shock or the glass to shatter suddenly Colin placed his finger-tip next to, and just touching his cousin's; but very nervously.

Almost immediately he took it off again.

'Don't we need to close the curtains or anything?'

'Don't be silly,' came the reply. 'Now come on, put your finger back on the glass and let's get started.'

He did so. There was a few moment's silence then Sally, in a different tone of voice, rather deeper, asked:

'Is anybody there?'

Colin's hand trembled slightly, but he controlled it.

'Is anybody there?'

Then in her normal voice to him: 'You're pressing too hard on the glass; it'll never move like that. Just touch it.'

Her cousin relaxed slightly letting his finger rest on the top.

'Is anybody there?'

They waited, each staring at the glass, then Sally suggested that they both ask – together.

'Is anybody there?' Colin's voice sounded very nervous and embarrassed.

'Louder,' hissed Sally.

'Is anybody there? . . . Is anybody there? . . . Is anybody there?'

Suddenly the glass began to move. Colin felt it almost becoming a live thing under his finger. It was actually moving, very hesitantly at first, feeling its way. Then, having described a small circle as if to examine all the letters, it began to move more steadily.

The cousins stared at the glass. Sally had done a seance before but then there had been lots of giggling with Tibs and Fran. This was completely different. Colin was too overwhelmed to think. He watched as the glass traced its erratic path across the table-top. *He* wasn't pushing it, and neither was Sally. Awkwardly, and with slight jerks at first, the glass moved – Colin glanced ahead, catching his breath when he realised 'Yes' was being indicated. 'Is anybody there?' they'd asked. 'Yes,' came the answer, clear as daylight. Somebody, a spirit, was there.

Having stopped at 'Yes' the glass went back to the centre of the circle. The cousins looked at each other and eventually Colin exclaimed:

'Gosh!'

'You see – it does work.'

'What do we do now Sally? Ask it, him, its name?'

'Yes'.

'On you go then'.

'What is your name?' Sally spoke in her different voice. With less awkwardness than before, the glass began to move. – Suddenly Sally interrupted:

'Before you tell us, go to the holy cross,' she commanded. Then, in an aside to her cousin, explained, 'You have got to get them to do that, or else things go wrong'

Colin nodded in agreement, but then asked: 'How do you mean, wrong?'

'Well if it refuses to go to the cross it means that the spirit is bad – then we stop, take our fingers off the glass and turn it the right way up to send the spirit back where it came from. After that we change places – you and me that is – and start again with a new spirit.'

'And if it does go to the holy cross?'

'Then there's no problem. You don't often get bad spirits – it's really just a safety precaution.' Sally was feeling very proud of her adult explanation, and of being taken so seriously that she hardly noticed the glass had been to the cross and was returning to the centre of the table.

'Do we ask it its name now?' suggested Colin.

'Yes.' Sally waited, half-expecting her cousin to put the question – then just as she was about to start, he did:

'Is anybody there?'

'We've done that already – the name, the name'

'Sorry, Sally. I got confused.' He paused and swallowed nervously. His arm was beginning to tire a little. He tried to relax it, then in a more serious tone of voice, asked very slowly as if speaking to someone who had to lip-read:

'What-is-your-name?'

Colin felt the glass tremble under his fingers then, after a pause, it began to move towards the letter 'M'.

Before he could stop himself he said 'Michael?'

The glass came to an abrupt halt and went to the 'No.' It then returned and proceeded as before towards the 'M'.

'M.M' Colin was puzzled.

Once more the glass stopped and went towards the 'No'.

'Oh, be quiet Colin – we'll never get anywhere at this rate. It wanted to start again from the beginning, that's all'.

Sally's observation was immediately confirmed by the spirit sending the glass straight to the 'Yes'.

'I'm sorry about this,' she apologised. 'Perhaps if you could begin for one last time, please. We won't interrupt, I promise.' She glared at her cousin who echoed: 'No we won't. I promise too'.

For the third time the glass went towards the 'M', paused for a moment, then went towards R, then D. It was now gliding smoothly and swiftly from letter to letter.

'MRDER?' exclaimed Colin suddenly. '– What kind of name
is that?' Though he was speaking to Sally, the glass stopped. It
stayed where it was as if waiting, with some irritation and
impatience, for Colin to finish his interruption.

'Maybe it means MURDER?' he ventured rather uncertainly.

At this the glass moved rapidly through a whole series of
letters 'ICANSPELL'. Sally laughed at her cousin's being told
off by a glass.

'I'm going to write all this down,' announced Colin taking a
pencil and some paper from his jacket pocket with his free hand.
The glass waited.

'MRDER' Colin spelled out. The glass then continued with
EKLAMB before returning to the centre.

Colin looked at the letters '– Maybe it's a spirit-name?' The
glass moved to 'No'. Suddenly Sally cried out:

'I've got it. Derek Lamb. Mr. Derek Lamb.' And the glass
moved to 'Yes'.

Thirty minutes later Derek had just begun to tell them of his
experiences in India when Colin interrupted:

'Your mother's coming, that's her car. I think we'd better
stop.'

'Why?' asked Sally.

'Just because we'd better,' came her cousin's reply.

'Don't be silly – there's nothing wrong.'

'I'm not being silly, it's – ' Colin hesitated, uncertain exactly
what to say. 'It's not that I want to stop,' he tried to explain,
excusing himself, '– but not with your mother here.'

The car-door slammed downstairs and he heard his aunt
coming into the house.

'We're stopping,' he said, asserting his two years' superiority.
Sally was glaring at him.

'No,' she said angrily.

'Yes. Goodbye till next time Derek.' Very quickly Colin took
his finger from the glass.

'You're rotten, Colin.' Sally stood up. Her cousin was already
picking up the pieces of paper.

'You're rotten, rotten, rotten.' She stormed out of the room. Methodically Colin put the pieces of paper in the glass, and then the glass out of sight in a cupboard.

During the day the weather had become very close and that night Sally couldn't sleep. She kept turning over in bed. The pillow was too warm, the sheets seemed to burn. She was thirsty. If I lived in India, she thought, it would be hot all the time – but I would have servants to bring me glasses of chilled lemonade. At school she had read about the British Empire and could picture sahibs and memsahibs sitting out on a verandah. She imagined herself in a large white dress and holding a white tasselled parasol. She liked parasols. Derek was sitting beside her.

She tried to imagine everything in colour, but the illustrations in her book had been in black and white. Gradually, however, she coloured-in some of the jungle near their clearing. Tree-trunks seemed like streaks of gold in the hot sun, standing in red sand. The Indians were brown – but that colour was difficult to hold onto and kept slipping into black or grey.

It was very difficult to concentrate, especially when she was so tired. The reds and golds seemed to wash over the whole scene quite freely according to where she focussed her attention. But whenever she returned to Derek he was exactly as before – tanned skin, in a white suit, and smiling.

Just as she was falling asleep she had the feeling that she really never did look away from him. Though she couldn't explain how, his presence was everywhere.

Next morning the cousins were taken for a run in the car to see an old church which, they were told, had been falling down for the last five hundred years. There was no roof, no windows, hardly any walls and the cafe was closed. Sally's parents thought some of the tombstones amusing – but at last they were returning home for lunch.

During the journey Colin kept touching a new spot which had begun to bud on his chin. That was after last night's activities – and he knew it. On his way upstairs to bed he had said over and over again that he wouldn't. And having decided to be so positive he had felt really happy for the first time in weeks. He washed, brushed his teeth, felt happy again, changed into his pyjamas, got into bed where he read two long chapters of 'The Old Curiousity Shop'. Then he put out the light.

And immediately he began to feel himself stiffen. He turned over, but he stiffened more. While lying on his back he tried to concentrate on little Nell and her grandfather's arrival at the inn. Dickens described a pot simmering full of gravy, meat and vegetables. Colin tried to remember what the inn was like, and all that was in the pot. He felt himself relaxing a little.

Yet no sooner was he aware of relaxing than he began to stiffen. He turned onto his front but that was even worse. Once more wouldn't matter, he thought.

Then he saw his future life stretch out before him – a broad and greasy highway of wanking and spots. *Now* was the time to decide for the rest of his life: either it would be spots and wanking or no-wanking and no-spots. There were arguments on both sides, but the latter at least held the possibility of something other than shame and loneliness. Once again his resolve was firm. He would not give way.

But another part of him was firm – and it too would not give way. In all good faith Colin tried to bend it, to buckle it, to force it to his will. It responded by becoming as correspondingly resistant. And when he turned onto his back it stood up straight like one of the trees in the garden. He felt its roots already reaching to every part of him. There had been six trees in the garden; before he could stop himself he had began counting them again. Over and over. Afterwards he had fallen asleep.

Neither of the cousins spoke very much as they were being driven home for lunch. Sally was thinking of Derek Lamb, and hoping her parents would go out that afternoon so they could have another seance. Colin, fingering the new spot on his chin, was reflecting upon his once-more blighted future.

After lunch Sally asked her cousin if he'd like to try the spirit-messages again.

'I suppose so,' was his enthusiastic response. At least it might take his mind off things. He had hardly spoken at all during the meal. He could feel *it* on his chin, clinging there like a swollen leech. If he tried hard enough he could even feel the blood beating through it. Surely they saw it – and they would know how it came to be there. Surely they too were disgusted. All through lunch he had hardly lifted his eyes from his plate.

'How do you know they won't be here?' he asked Sally.

'Oh, I heard them talking about some car museum,' she explained.

'OK,' he agreed, '– once they've gone.'

From then on, whenever an outing was suggested the cousins tried to make excuses to stay at home. Having heard the car start they would begin clearing the table and laying-out the letters. By the time it turned into the main road they were already seated, fingers on the tumbler, asking together: 'Is anybody there?'

Into herself Sally would say, 'Let it be Derek.' Sometimes it was – more often, however, a succession of dead relatives and strangers lead them up and down various by-ways of the past. From some who had crossed in the 'Mayflower' and claimed in the same breath, so to speak, to have ridden with Jesse James – to others who stated they had lived and died quietly: a seamstress in Bradford, an Edinburgh tea-merchant.

Colin took notes, finding refuge in this patient occupation. His mind was calmed as he listened to the gentle rumbling sound made by the glass as it slid across the table, and as he wrote down concientiously, letter by letter, the messages spelt out for them. Most of these were commonplace and reassuring: 'I am happy now, though I miss TV.' He came almost to treasure their banality. For a few hours he forgot his self-disgust, and that was enough.

Sally's parents seemed pleased to be left to go off by themselves looking at more churches and museums. The only complaints were of the usual kind: 'I thought I told you to lock the back-door,' or 'Sally, have you borrowed my needle-case again?' The usual complaints – but made much more often. It was better when they were working, Sally thought to herself, for then they were less bored and irritable.

One afternoon when Colin and her father had gone fishing and her mother had gone shopping, Sally remained in the house by herself but couldn't settle. She wandered through the rooms, went upstairs, then back downstairs. She decided to make some tea, boiled the water and then changed her mind. She wandered upstairs again.

If only she could have a seance by herself, she thought, but was certain it wouldn't work – Tibs and Fran had said so. And even if it did she would probably get some ancient old great-aunt. What she wanted was a seance of just herself and Derek. But she knew it wouldn't work.

She took out the glass and the pieces of paper – these were already curling at the edges, quite worn and smudged. She must make some new ones soon. It was rather strange, sitting there by herself with her finger only on the glass. She felt uncomfortably aware of being alone in the large empty house. He arm seemed to ache very quickly. Her voice, when asking 'Is anybody there?' seemed almost to be speaking to her. She shivered.

Outside, the sun shone strongly and a shaft of light lay across the carpet at her feet. She glanced at it, shivered again, then brought her attention back to the glass on the table.

'Is anybody there?' she asked several times, her voice becoming quieter with each successive silence. Gradually she began repeating quite calmly and steadily, 'Is anybody there?'

At last she sat without speaking, her finger motionless on the glass, her restlessness gone. She sensed Derek's presence in a silence composed of reds and golds. She lifted her finger from the glass – all *that* was unnecessary now.

They stood together looking across an immense plain where a heat-haze shimmered. She was dressed in white, but whenever Derek turned towards her she felt the thin cotton become drenched in colours of the distant landscape. The air was difficult to breath, windless and heavy – but she was no longer afraid.

She was dressed in colours only, colours that fell away at his glance. And it was his voice she heard whisper the command:

'experience', that made the entire continent dissolve into her as she lay on the couch by the open window.

Sometime afterwards, hearing her mother's car turn off the main road, she got up, checked her appearance in the mirror, put away the glass and pieces of paper – then went downstairs to greet her.

The cousins continued their seances. By the second week, however, Sally was beginning to feel uneasy: things were indeed going missing, sometimes to turn-up in the unlikeliest places; windows and doors that had been well-secured were found open. Then one morning, three out of a set of six wine-glasses were discovered smashed on the drinks-tray. Accident or not, her mother said, whoever had done it had made no attempt to clear up the broken glass.

Later that day her mother returned from shopping to find the remaining three glasses smashed and the pieces left once more on the tray. Also, a vase had been broken and the flowers scattered across the room. The cousins were nowhere to be seen.

That afternoon Sally and Colin had been listening to the reminiscences of Elizabeth Mann, a lady-in-waiting to the wife of George II. Suddenly from downstairs came a series of crashes and the sound of breaking glass.

'I thought you said they were out,' accused Colin.

'They are.'

At the noise the tumbler, which had been moving in hesitant jerks for several moments, stopped altogether. Sally took her finger from it and listened, but heard nothing else.

'Probably just the wind,' remarked Colin adding, 'Maybe I should go down to have a look.'

'It's hardly worth it,' commented Sally as casually as she could. 'There's nothing now – let's get on with the seance. They'll be back soon.'

'Only take a few minutes,' said Colin getting up.

'Don't bother please.' Sally tried not to sound pleading; she placed her finger back on the glass.

Colin shrugged his shoulders and sat down again.

'OK, let's start again.'

They began together: 'Is anybody there? . . .Is anybody there?' Suddenly the glass moved, but so erratically as to make it difficult for them to keep their fingers in place. Then it swept round the table in wide circles until it stopped abruptly at the letter D.

'D-' Colin said aloud, writing it down.

Instead of returning to the centre, however, the glass cut straight into the circle of letters and began ploughing its way through them, sweeping the bits of paper to one side. Everything was happening too quickly for the children to think to take their fingers away. The glass, which had begun circling much faster now, suddenly swerved as though to free itself, then shot out over the edge of the table, smashing to pieces on the floor.

There was a moment's horrified pause, then Sally burst into tears.

'Don't be scared, Sal,' Colin's voice wavered.

'I'm not – I'm not,' she sobbed. A few minutes later the two of them ran downstairs and out of the house.

Colin's bedroom window overlooked the garden with the six trees. As he undressed and got into bed that night he began thinking of numbers. Recently they had begun to fascinate him, especially prime numbers. All the rest seemed flawless, predictable and yet insubstantial – they would come apart at a touch into multiples of two, three and primes. The latter, like 7, 11, 13 for example, felt charged with mystery and revealed nothing of their origins. Each had a different character: 7 felt rather sluggish whereas 11 would leap almost effortlessly over all the stepping-stones of 22, 33, 44 etc. as far as he could see.

Colin had had no new spots for several days and was feeling much happier again. Every so often the desire to wank would occur. He might be opening a door or brushing his teeth, perhaps, but now he simply started trying to work out higher and higher primes – and gradually the desire would go. His problems were solved for he knew that the series of prime numbers was infinite – easily enough to take care of all the times he would feel like wanking in his life! And – no wanking, no spots. Ah, life was good!

However, negative numbers disturbed him. Their magnitude and yet sudden impossibility almost had him in tears. What region was theirs? When he seemed about to grasp physically the idea of such a region, it was lost once more. Instead he lay in bed imagining the house not as a place of chairs, tables and stairways but as a complex of interlocking numbers. He considered the unphysical nature of the wood and stone that made up the building and its contents, the pattern of things. The vase and scattered flowers were disturbances in this, like a repeating decimal that had somehow become flawed – to resolve not as a vase of flowers but as smashed pottery, scattered petals and stems.

The more he thought as he lay there, the more miraculous it seemed that the room remained as two chairs, a table, a bed, wardrobe and carpet. Why didn't everything fall apart into its lowest common denominator: the glass and putty no longer hold to the window-frame; the clock-parts disengage; *The Old Curiousity Shop* become so many hundreds of loose pages strewn across the floor?

He felt it could happen at any minute. If he panicked, there would be chaos. Already the window was rattling and he was certain he heard the clock ticking unevenly. He began counting to hold everything together.

Slowly the numbers formed in his mind. One, two, three – very carefully he groped his way, one wrong turn and he was certain the entire room would shudder then give way on all sides. He reached ten laboriously. Then twenty. Thirty. He was cautious at prime numbers feeling a strange power exerted on him to linger there.

Gradually he progressed through the forties and fifties. He lay counting desperately into himself – he could hear that the window had stopped rattling, but he had to keep going. Seventies, eighties, nineties: the greater the number he reached the more steady would things remain, and, feeling more confident, he began counting faster.

As he did so, he felt himself stiffening. He grew harder and harder as the numbers fell away at greater speed. 150, 160 – the room was quite stable now, but still he kept going further and growing stiffer. He had to stop counting – but not yet.

Then he realised that if he reached a prime everything would be alright – any other number would fall apart immediately and so return the room to chaos. A prime number was safe – he could release himself there. But the higher he counted the further apart these numbers became, and he could not hold out much longer being so stiff and expectant. 218, 219, 220 – his mind raced ahead searching out the next prime. 223? – but he wasn't sure. 229? – that seemed more likely. But he felt he was going to burst apart before reaching it. 225, 226 – hold, hold he was saying to himself. 227, 228, 229 . . .

During the night Colin woke up to repeat the exercise, reaching the number 371. Afterwards the room felt very stable and he slept well.

Sally woke up during the night. Her room was very warm and though it was in complete darkness she sensed the colours there, radiating heat as they merged and separated around her. She didn't turn away. The covers slid from the bed; her cotton night-dress lifted easily.

She lay naked aware only of the reds and golds concealed in the darkness, pressing down onto her.

Afterwards she fell into a light sleep, to waken later and drowsily pull back the blankets.

Next morning Colin got up early and looked in the mirror expecting the worst after the previous night's fall from grace. He knew his face well. Where each spot budded, blossomed and burst was such familiar territory that he could have drawn a relief-map showing the current situation, complete with a colour-coded key-chart to indicate likely areas of future development.

And so there was no doubt in his mind when he looked and saw – no change. A double-wank and no spots! Briefly the thought passed through his mind that there had been no time for any effect. He dismissed this immediately and with scorn. 'Sucks to Mike,' he said, winking to himself in the mirror. He started down the stairs two at a time.

His aunt was coming up, she seemed agitated as if she had been crying. Carry straight on through the hall and out the front door, she told him. She was just going to call Sally – and on no account, she added, was he to go into the kitchen.

Colin could see his uncle standing at the front door, holding it open. He had begun making his way across the hall when, from the corner of eye, he noticed the kitchen door swing open slightly. At the same time he was aware of his uncle calling and gesturing towards him.

It might have been the comparative darkness of the hall, but the kitchen seemed unnaturally bright. He felt his uncle's hand on his shoulder just as he reached the door. He began to struggle and his uncle had to force him to remain still.

Colin turned on him in a fury kicking, biting and punching his way out of his uncle's grasp. His uncle hit back. Colin tasted blood in his mouth. Within moments, however, his uncle had manoeuvered so that he stood between Colin and the kitchen; and gradually he began to force the boy back into the hall.

Colin ran upstairs, passing his aunt on the way, and went straight into the room where he and Sally held their seances.

It was too warm in here. The curtains were closed but sunlight seeped weakly into the room. When his eyes had become accustomed to the half-light he saw the seance table set up with his cousin seated behind it. He took the chair opposite her. And immediately he placed his finger on the glass the air around him became filled with the sound of people crying out their grief.

Colin put his hands to his ears, but already the clamour had entered him. At the same time he could sense the angles in the room coming apart: the floor and the walls were buckling.

'Is anybody there?' the cousins began when Colin had replaced his finger on the glass. A mirror on the wall opposite had ceased to reflect – showing only a hardly perceptible blue, framed by drifting smoke.

'Is anybody there?' The clamour was growing louder inside him – some voices seemed to be crying for forgiveness, others for release. The outlines of the furniture were becoming vague.

'Is anybody there?'

The glass began to move. Intently the cousins watched it make its very laborious way around the table, as though it were discovering the alphabet.

Behind him Colin could feel the room sliding towards chaos. Soon there would be only his cousin Sally and himself – and these colours he could now see slanting across her.

Finally the glass went towards 'Yes'. Colin saw Sally's lips move but he could hear nothing. He felt his mind invaded by grief; and then he realised his own voice was asking something, he could feel his lips move, but could hear nothing.

The glass began again. By now, however, the pieces of paper and the table itself were appearing less substantial. The letters had completely faded yet the glass continued spelling out its message with the remaining blanks.

Hoping to arrest and steady this disintegration Colin began to count. In his panic, however, he blundered from number to number – too confused and frightened to keep to any sequence. The noise inside him was deafening, and he could not tell whether he was screaming these random numbers out loud or not.

His cousin Sally – her face, her shoulders, her arms – was becoming unrecognisable, distorted. Her expression altered moment by moment from sudden anguish to an ecstacy as the colours caressed and seemed almost to cut into her.

All at once Colin sensed the despairing voices inside him resolve into one cry of final longing; within Sally the colours merged suddenly into a light so blinding he had to close his eyes. His last thought as everything around and within him began to shudder was that they too, his cousin and himself, were about to disintegrate – yet until the last moment he could feel their fingertips still touch.

A Short Biography

Bernard lived in a flat that overlooked the park. On Tuesday and Thursday evenings between seven and nine, other times by appointment, he was available for private consultation as a handwriting-expert. His charges were modest – it was really no more than a hobby.

One night he seemed unable to concentrate. He glanced again at the clock on the mantlepiece – ten to eight. The woman sitting opposite him was well-dressed though rather weary-looking; he guessed she was in her mid-forties. During the last few minutes her embarrassment had increased. Bernard smiled encouragingly at her and waited. Her jewellery was the wrong colour.

'I've brought some examples of –,' she was saying. Bernard's attention wandered back to the clock, then to a china robin-redbreast a few inches to the left. One of the legs was broken-off, he would have to fix it. He tried remembering where he had put the chipped piece. In the blue vase? The cutlery drawer, perhaps? The woman was pulling out papers from her bag. Letters, small notes, cards. She was starting to apologise for the muddle. Everything, of course, was very personal. She seemed on the verge of tears.

There is no hurry, Bernard said into himself; if she wants to cry, let her cry. There is no hurry.

He took the letters first, and laid out a few of them on his desk, smoothing them flat. Then the cards and two of the notes. He said nothing for several minutes while he glanced over the pieces of paper. Everything was signed Stephen, or simply S. The writing was untidy with frequent spelling mistakes; the paper rather dog-eared and crumpled, presumably with frequent re-reading.

Bernard usually had three or four clients on each evening. Sometimes they came in shyly, sometimes brusquely, and either they talked far too much with an excited nervousness, or else they said almost nothing. Having given him whatever they wished examined, sooner or later they looked at him and asked, 'Well?' – sometimes adding, 'You can tell me the truth, I must know.' The woman opposite would be no exception. Bernard wondered, as he worked his way through the papers before him, whether she would ask – say the actual words – 'Does he love me?' She appeared so unhappy, she might.

She was looking away from him now, at the ornaments on the mantlepiece – things in pottery, glass and silverplate. Nothing valuable, just the bits and pieces accumulated over the years. Some were gifts from clients. Bernard saw her smile briefly – she must have noticed the robin-redbreast perched miraculously on its one leg. A pleasing smile, spontaneous and quite of a moment's forgetfulness. Would he see the same, he wondered, in the manner she gathers up these papers before leaving – in a gesture that betrays she knows it hardly matters whether Stephen loves her or not?

Bernard opened the right-hand drawer of his desk and took out a magnifying glass. As he bent over the letters he could sense the woman's agitation return. She leant forward.

'Do you mind if I smoke?' she asked.Bernard shook his head and, without glancing up, replied, 'Not at all, please carry on'.

The letters expressed a confusion of promises, explanations and apologies. As was his custom he did not examine the sentences sequentially but glanced here and there at random. To rest his eyes he looked up for a moment. It was five past eight.

Bernard was not unhappy – at least he didn't think so, though sometimes it was difficult to tell. Earlier he had glanced up at the clock to check whether or not there was time for a cup of tea before the consultations began. He had been half-listening to the radio and half day-dreaming as he watched a trickle of tea rising slowly up into the sugar cube he'd placed on the spoon.

No, he was not unhappy; but later, when trying to describe what had happened at this point, he used the words 'anxiety' and 'fear'. It had felt as if some moments of his life had taken place only inside himself – and nowhere else. He had been staring absently at the teaspoon he was holding when, all at once, he became certain that if he let go, the spoon would remain there – balanced impossibly upon the rim of the cup. The clock hands also, he realised suddenly, though correctly positioned at ten to seven, were in fact positioned without any significance – and would remain so until by an effort of his will, their significance was restored.

A biographer would have seen nothing to remark upon. For Bernard, however, it seemed as though these commonplace words, 'fireplace', 'radio' and 'desklight', had been briefly written in an unfamiliar hand. And, a moment later, he could not remember what he had just read there as, with a clatter, the teaspoon fell into the saucer, the fire continued to burn, the radio to play and the desklight to shine. Some tea was spilt onto his suit – and he had only just enough time to change before his first client arrived.

'Well?' the woman began, regarding him anxiously as he took up one of the pieces of paper, a note scrawled on a blank restaurant bill. He read: 'Don't smile, look over to me sometimes. S.', then he replaced the note on his desk.

'Can you tell –,' she continued hesitantly. 'That is, now that you've seen these, Mr Lawrence, do you think – ?'. Bernard gestured that there was no need to finish. He seems very kind, the woman thought to herself as though noticing him for the first time.

After fifteen years experience Bernard knew exactly how to phrase his reply. He proceeded to demonstrate his conclusions with reference to the way certain alterations in hand-pressure, letter-height, steadiness etc., betrayed not only the writer's emotional state but also his response to that state, with regard to the recipient – for example, a desire for concealment or emphasis. Bernard went into detail knowing quite well that the woman opposite, who was nodding her head every few seconds, was taking in nothing of these proofs and illustrations.

She left at eight-twenty. Afterwards he saw two other people one of whom was obviously a little disturbed and, Bernard suspected, had himself written these extremely abusive letters.

That night Bernard lay in bed unable to sleep. He switched on the light for a moment – it was almost two o'clock. He turned over and began thinking of the woman who had brought the love letters. Of course 'Stephen' didn't love her, she must have known that already; but as a study of the handwriting alone could be expected neither to confirm nor deny this absolutely, there was now a measure of doubt for her, of hope in fact. She had gone away well pleased.

He must have fallen asleep for when he next switched on the light it was a quarter to five. He felt relaxed and very warm, the slightest movement seemed to make him even more comfortable. In the distance a train whistled. Knowing he was about to fall asleep again Bernard closed his eyes and found himself thinking of the abusive letters. – And suddenly, in his drowsy state, they seemed to have been addressed to him and told, he felt sure, truths of his own life. Each was like a short biography, written in a tone of accusation – and scarcely legible, save for the word 'Yes' written clearly here and there as though in lieu of more conventional punctuation.

The Sound of a Gamelan Orchestra

For the third time that day Matthew considered the mobile of delicately worked glass and copper-wire. Then, leaning close, he breathed upon it – creating the slightest whispering noise and a fragmented spectrum. Gradually the condensation evaporated leaving colourless glass and copper. More than forty years ago he had called this sculpture 'Here I am' – not the kind of title he would use nowadays.

He had been returning from a party about 5 a.m. one summer's morning, his mind filled with the girl he had just left. The deserted streets, the parked cars, the iron railings, the noise of the dawn chorus – all were taking place elsewhere. She alone was happening – and forty years later he could still remember how touching her crinkled red hair was like drawing his hand through fire.

He was so filled with her he wanted to run, to exhaust himself. He wanted to tell someone, to announce her to the whole world. A telephone-box stood at the next corner. Perhaps he could call his friend Colin just to say, 'It's me, Matthew, and I'm so very happy here in the big, empty streets at five in the morning'. But no, either Colin wouldn't answer, would hang-up, or, at best, demand explanations – and there was nothing more he wanted to say. Instead, without anger, he kicked in each of the bottom panes of glass. Afterwards he began walking home at a normal pace.

But only for a few yards. He stopped, then returned to look at what he had done. A few moments later he was gathering up the fragments of glass, cautiously prising out the jagged edge pieces that remained in the frames. Though he was very careful he cut his fingers several times and, to reduce the bleeding, had to carry the glass in his upturned hands which he held just above shoulder-height. This was very tiring and every so often he was forced to rest his elbows against a wall or pillar-box.

It took nearly an hour to reach home, by which time his arms ached unbearably. He did not go to bed however. Instead, having taken all the glass in one hand, with the other he pulled at the top blanket and spread it on the floor as best he could. Then, thankfully, he laid the broken glass upon it.

Matthew put the kettle on to boil then rolled up his sleeves and washed the blood from his hands and arms. When the water was ready he poured it into a basin and began painstakingly to clean each piece of glass.

Apart from two very quick breaks for something to eat he worked continuously through the day until, by the early hours of the following morning, he had finished. Three of his flatmates were still awake and Matthew can still remember their delight at breathing upon his sculpture. Afterwards he had slept for twelve hours.

Matthew replaced 'Here I am' carefully in its position beside some other pieces on a polished wooden shelf and returned to his workbench. This stood in the centre of his studio, the upper storey of a house he himself had designed. It was very quiet here – a good place to spend a working winter, he had thought when first visiting the Alpine village by chance some twenty years ago.

And he always had plenty of work. At other times of the year his base was a large flat in London near the British Museum; from there he would travel all over the world lecturing, exhibiting and being celebrated. At the moment, however, he was engaged on a small carving – a private commission he had felt certain he would enjoy working on.

His tools were laid out neatly on the table – the various chisels, knives, files and sandpapers he would require. He had spent some considerable time meditating upon the piece and choosing the appropriate wood. From the very start he knew exactly what he wished to do.

Why then was it taking so long? For nearly five weeks he had been fiddling about with this lump of wood, staring at it for hours at a time. He would sit out on the verandah looking at the clouds or at the wind disturbing snow-patterns on the roofs; yet he was always aware of the wood his hands held in his lap. Exploring it, feeling it, caressing it almost, his fingers never stopped trying to coax some life out of, or into, its deadness. And it was not just this piece, he knew; for the last few years he had been struggling without release. Not work, but careful labour.

His sculptures were admired not only by the public, but by many of his fellow artists – a rare distinction. Women, and sometimes men, beautiful, crazy, understanding, gave themselves to him as if they might then sense something they felt denied. To the curious he would answer, '– imagination, persistence and persistence'. They would smile and shake their heads.

Matthew picked up the piece of wood and began sandpapering a ragged edge he had cut in a moment's irritation two days ago. He felt more peaceful now, smoothing, polishing. Every few minutes he stopped and carefully blew away the accumulated dust. Then he resumed his patient work.

What time is it? he wondered. If it was three o'clock then he could go downstairs and ask Anna if she would like to come for a walk with him. Having been in his studio since eight-thirty that morning he had put in a good six hours, allowing for lunch, which sanctioned a clear conscience for the rest of the day. As there were some people coming to dinner he and Anna would discuss possible menus during the walk before going down to the village to buy what extras might be required. It was leaving things rather to the last minute, but dinner parties were often better like that, less formal.

It was just two-thirty. Another half-hour still to go. Matthew sandpapered for a few minutes more then, walking out onto the open balcony, held the wood up above eye-level to catch the full light. He kept his arms raised as long as he could, turning his hands to see every side, but nothing happened. He returned indoors, and having replaced the lump of wood on the bench, sat down in his armchair.

Perhaps he shouldn't have come here at all. He was a sociable man and enjoyed the stimulation of fellow artists dropping in from time to time to talk shop. Whereas, up here in the mountains, all he ever heard was the soft rattling of cow-bells from across the valley. He could hardly blame the cow-bells or Mont Blanc – yet he worked as hard as he ever had, perhaps even harder, and nothing happened.

He sat listening to the cow-bells and pretended instead he was listening to a gamalan orchestra. He had heard one while visiting Bali a few years ago, and the sound was really quite similar. His host had given him the captivating description of the orchestra as being, in fact, but one instrument – rather like an immense piano played on by twenty players at once. As he listened it seemed that suddenly he was hearing the cowbells' sound as shaped in a continuously varying counterpoint to the almost mystic relationship between the players – and between each player and the gamalan.

Excitedly, Matthew picked up the pencil and pad of paper from the small table beside him and began sketching the sound of this gamalan orchestra. He encouraged himself by muttering under his breath, 'Yes, that's it ...No, not quite... Again.' He tried sketch after sketch, '– better, better'. Each seemed to fail differently though he felt he was getting closer. 'No, no... Almost,' he said and tried again.

After nearly twenty attempts he sat quite still. Then, without rising from his chair, gathered up the various sheets that lay within reach. He glanced through them one by one, slowly; but there was nothing – just meaningless lines, curves and smudges. He remained where he was for several minutes staring at the pages on his lap.

It would be after three now. He got up intending to have one more look at the piece he was trying to work on before going downstairs. Instead, for the fourth time that day, he found himself examining 'Here I am'. Affectionately he picked it up then leant close to breathe upon it and hear its whispered reply. He carried it over to the verandah to enjoy more fully the clear mountain light breaking and reforming inside it.

The condensation was evaporating gradually, and the colours

fading. He raised it higher – his arms began to tremble, yet always there seemed the possibility of another shred of colour if he tilted the piece differently. His whole body began shaking with the strain of holding it up to the light. He became exhilerated. He became certain that something was about to happen. Something miraculous. Suddenly the effort was too great – the sculpture fell to the floor and shattered.

Matthew staggered against the work table. He rested there for a few minutes to recover his breath. There was broken glass everywhere and he could see at a glance the work was beyond repair. Absently he began picking up some of the pieces – it was then that he realised he was crying.

That was how she found him, Anna was telling their friends that evening when her husband was out of the room making coffee: on his knees amid the fragments of his first sculpture, and in tears.

Matthew, meanwhile, had set the water to boil and stepped out onto the verandah. It pleased him to remain there for a few minutes, listening to the soft rattle of the cow-bells coming from across the valley through the clear night air. It pleased him for the first time in years.

Taking Tea

The old woman had mumbled something about 'three weeks' and continued stirring her tea. – Or perhaps Martin hadn't heard correctly, she seemed to relish the noise of the traffic and every few minutes would give her complete attention to some car or lorry that was going past. As the two windows looking onto the street were wide-open Martin had followed very little of the conversation. He continued sipping his tea and nodded once more.

Nothing seemed to have altered since his last visit though perhaps the room was dustier, it was difficult to tell. The grand piano was still on its side propped against the wall, beside it a large and ornate harmonium. Standing some three feet away from the far wall was a bright blue kitchen-cabinet in front of which were stacked several columns of plastic flower-pots with earth spilled around them. Yellowed newspapers were scattered here and there.

Though the room was obviously not arranged for habitation Martin could see that the old lady had begun to take her meals here for dirty plates lay on the mantlepiece and some were piled on a small table beside her. Grey-looking armchairs, in two rows of three, faced into the room. He had once sat on one of them and immediately felt his mouth going dry – at the moment even the tea was beginning to taste dusty.

After a short pause Martin prompted, '– "Three weeks" you were saying.'

'Only a suggestion, I leave it entirely up to you,' she remarked. The young man's reply was completely ignored however, a motorcycle heing revved up outside. She motioned him to be silent.

'Triumph 500cc twin, a quite distinctive sound. Can you hear,' she shouted at Martin, 'that rattling noise, like milk-crates? – The tappets. A give-away.' She smiled and poured more tea. 'Daniel had a Triumph,' she added. '– Is that enough milk?'

'Yes, thank you. Three weeks –'

'– and he was forever taking it to bits. Not that I minded, but these bits – and some of them were quite large bits – kept finding their way into the hall, the kitchen and then upstairs until we ended-up with a complete crankshaft, stripped down of course, in the bedroom. It was the newspapers that bothered me, though it was me who insisted upon them to catch the oil – made the place look so gypsy-like.'

'Oh, yes.' Martin's attention had wandered again.

'But it all helps doesn't it?' she stated abruptly. Martin agreed uncertainly. He had been thinking of Kathy's left hand, quite brown with the sun, placed gently against his elbow. She had been wanting to point out something to him – what was it? He was trying to remember where they had been when a sudden silence in the old lady's talk recalled him to the room.

A large gilt mirror leant against the nearby wall. Martin could see himself and the old woman there, taking tea.

'Three weeks –,' she began again, then broke off suddenly. 'We don't live forever, you know, but spend our entire lives acting as if we ought to.'

At this observation Martin brightened-up immediately. He was eighteen years old and once in the abstract felt on much surer ground.

'– But don't you think,' he interrupted eagerly, 'it's not so much a question of how long, rather – one might say – it's almost as if one indeed *does* live forever, sometimes, that is. When one –'

Turning to face her he suddenly caught sight of his reflection turning in the mirror. Momentarily he lost the direction of his argument.

'– That is, I mean,' he stammered trying to recover himself and continue. 'It is as if sometimes – not often – whole moments seem to fill –' he was back on course now, 'yes, whole moments seem to fill the entire universe, and are themselves filled by it.' He leant back in his seat.

'Yes, I suppose they are,' replied the old woman glancing towards one of the open windows. '– And how's Kathy?' she asked suddenly. Martin, who had been warming to his subject, replied rather abruptly, 'Oh, fine. Fine – same as usual'.

There was a moment's silence, then he leant forward, 'What I mean is – '

'– She seemed a nice girl,' the old woman commented. 'Quite beautiful in her own way. Don't you think?'

'Oh, yes.' Maybe it was about time to leave, he thought. Kathy had arranged to meet him at five – he had no watch and couldn't see a clock in the room. She hated being kept waiting and, as things weren't going too well at the moment, he wanted to be there on time. 'Yes, she's a really nice girl,' he added. Of course, they had been outdoors, near the sea. He remembered now. They had stopped during a walk when she had placed her hand on his arm – to point out a seabird, perhaps?

'You must bring her next time – I've some old things she might like, nowadays young girls seem to prefer wearing old-fashioned clothes. And, goodness knows, I've plenty of these!' She laughed then continued after a pause, 'Not the men so much, I've noticed. No spats and boaters. Pity. You'd look rather fetching in spats, stripes and a boater, Martin.'

Yes, they had been by the sea – earlier in the summer. They had taken a high path above the dunes when suddenly she'd stopped and pointed to the edge of a field where there was a reddish smear of poppies, or was it an abandoned tractor? – he couldn't remember. But the touch of her hand on his arm – all its sudden intimacy was flooding into him as he sat in that dusty room.

'Don't you know what spats are?' the old lady was asking.

'Pardon? Spats?' repeated Martin.

With great deliberation, saying nothing, she lifted a corner of the table cloth and looked underneath.

'Gym-shoes!' she observed with scorn. Martin, rather confused, could only agree.

'I run a lot' he explained weakly then glanced round the room once more in case there was clock he had somehow missed. The two of them sat without speaking for several moments.

'Well,' said Martin, 'I think it's time I wasn't here. I'm meeting Kathy out from her exams.'

The old woman made no response. Thinking maybe she hadn't heard, a lorry having cut-off part of his announcement, Martin began again:'I think that perhaps I'd better –'.

'Yes, yes,' she interrupted. 'Of course; never keep a lady waiting.'

Martin laughed, then realised that the old woman hadn't even smiled. She wasn't looking at him, her fingers had begun picking bits of fluff from her jersey. Martin stood up awkwardly.

'It's been nice seeing you again,' he stated. 'Really.'

'Yes,' she repeated, 'very nice'.

'Shall I close the windows before I go? It will be getting cold soon.'

'The windows?' the old woman seemed confused for a moment. '– Oh, the windows. No, leave them just now. I'll manage – don't you worry about me.'

Martin came round and bent over to kiss her on the forehead. As he was straightening up he saw himself in the mirror once more – his gestures parodying, and yet at the same time catching him to life.

'Good-bye then,' he said too quickly.

'Good-bye, Martin.'

When he reached the door leading to the hall Martin turned to give a wave and a smile. At the same moment a taxi braked outside. The old lady glanced towards the window. Martin stood uncertainly at the door waiting for her to look round and see him. He waited as long as he could.

Only when the old woman heard the front door close after her visitor did she stop staring out of the window. She remained in her chair for a few minutes until she felt ready to carry the tea-things through to the kitchen.

The Polish Princess

Sooner or later I will begin telling Tommy and his lodger about the Polish Princess, but for the moment it's good simply to lean out into the street and breathe. His room is stifling. Even on a day as hot as this he wouldn't think of opening his window.

Tommy's place is a bedsit with two beds hardly three feet apart, a low table set between them and no chairs. The table always seems laid for a meal and the meal always seems half-eaten. Being thrifty he dines by candlelight only when absolutely necessary, the electricity having been long since cut-off. A similar economy has meant that the paraffin heater doubles as a stove. As he is quite a neat man, even when drunk, the room is filthy but not untidy. His lodger, however, is filthy, untidy and talks in his sleep. Even when he is awake he talks as if he is talking in his sleep. Tommy remarked to me once that having him as a lodger was like having a radio he could never completely turn-off.

'I was in the Market Bar last night,' Tommy began. 'I had a nip, Dave a half-and-half, Margo a campari – no, a rum and coke – and Brenda a gin. I got the first round.'

That must have been quite early for it was just after nine when I saw him escorting a woman called Brenda up here to his room: two people, both at least sixty years old, struggling upstairs separately to damp sheets, a paraffin heater and a broken skylight.

Brenda came to rest near my door just as I was returning from a visit to my daughter who lives over in Stockbridge. I was soaked through. Brenda needed another drink to reach another floor, she said. All I wanted was to dry myself, then get into bed with a cup of tea and something good to read. She began on the next flight but obviously wouldn't make it. Rain ran down the steps. I was about to open my door when she sat down. Her head leant against the wall with a sudden crack that seemed to split the building.

'I'd forgotten all about him, of course,' Tommy said to me pointing to the lodger who was still sleeping though it was afternoon. '– Worse than when I was a kid and bringing women back with the old man still at home. Look at him. All he does these days is sweat over torn-out pictures. He gives them names and talks to them.'

I had watched Brenda's hand clutching at the falling water to pull herself up. The stair-lights dazzled her, and when she shut her eyes the water whirled round and down into the basement. Looking up I saw that Tommy was waiting on the next floor so I helped her to her feet. She made the rest of the way herself.

Not that she seemed to notice the lodger at first, Tommy told me. She complained that the glare from the streetlights hurt her eyes and couldn't he do something about it? Standing on a tea-chest at one window and then on the lodger's bed at the other, he spent the next few minutes fixing bits of towel and newspaper to the curtain-rail. Meanwhile Brenda had passed out and wet his bed.

'I couldn't even move her,' he said as he bent down to rinse two tea-cups in a basin of water under the table. 'Don't like mixing my drinks,' he joked. He shook them dry, cleared a small space on the table then poured us each a Scotsmac.

The lodger stirred restlessly, raised his head from the pillow and stared at us, his eyes wide open. Then he sank back on the bed.

'He can smell it even in his sleep,' remarked Tommy.

'Didn't he notice anything last night?' I asked.

'Didn't he just!' he replied unhappily, '– on top form he was. On top form,' he repeated, glaring in the direction of his lodger.

'Anyway – ' he raised his tea-cup, 'to better days – and nights.' We drank. The first Scotsmac is always the worst so we downed it quickly and refilled.

'What hapened next?' I prompted, '– with Brenda?'

'Well she – ' he began hesitatingly. Then he looked straight at me. 'You see,' he continued, 'I went to sleep for a while, then woke up with this whisky hard-on. Know what I mean? A real dinger – and at our time of life we've got to make the most of it.' He laughed and had another drink.

'But did she come over with the goods? – No chance,' he continued. 'Started on instead about what a bad mother her daughter was. All these grandchildren she had that didn't even know how to brush their teeth. A fascinating conversation – as you can imagine.'

I noticed that the lodger was now sitting up in bed and looking at his hands.

Tommy continued, 'So I'm still lying there with this whisky hard-on, agreeing with whatever she's saying, being sympathetic and understanding, you name it; and all the time trying to get in this way or that. Back or front, I didn't care – I just wanted in. 'What did I think of her daughter? Brenda asks me. Bloody rotten and ungrateful, I answers patting her back to show sincerity and slide the hand down a bit.'

By now the lodger had brought his fingers up close to his face and seemed to be examining the spaces between them.

'Mind you,' Tommy was saying, 'I was getting worried that the whisky might die on me – like Moses in sight of the Promised Land. Another drink?' he asked hospitably.

He refilled the tea-cups. I knew this would be much better – the sickliness and bitterness would either have reached a compromise or, at the very least, have become resigned to each other.

'To the Promised Land,' I suggested, and we drank. '– And did you get there?'

The lodger laughed suddenly. His face was partly hidden behind his outstretched fingers but I could see that he was looking at us.

'Shut up.' Tommy snapped at him.

'I know he had a visitor here last night,' the man in the bed said to me. 'I live here, you see. I'm Tommy's lodger.'

'Pleased to meet you,' I replied as if we'd never seen each other before. Though it was already very close in the room he put on a jumper over his pyjamas. He remained in bed.

'Go back to sleep,' said Tommy.

The lodger paid no attention.

'Yes,' he continued, 'He'd somebody's granny in here last night. And got sweet FA I can tell you. I heard him trying. I was lying here for hours wishing even more than him that she'd give him a bit – then we could all get some sleep.'

Then he turned to face Tommy. 'You didn't get anything. A pity. And you'd probably spent my whole week's rent on getting her filled up beforehand. Anyway I got rid of her for you.'

'Too right you did,' said Tommy dejectedly.

'Scared the shits out of her!' the lodger laughed.

I felt it was time to leave and made as though to stand up.

'Don't bother yourself,' the lodger gestured me to be still. 'Sit down. Pay no attention to us. – We're just having a bit of fun. Pour him another drink Tommy.'

Without saying anything I crossed the room a few moments later, opened the window and leant out.

The air feels cool and refreshing. Another day is finishing. The street is nearly empty and at the sudden noise of a shop-blind being raised several sea-gulls rise startled, then settle a few yards further away. When I turn back into the room I know what will happen: I will roll-up my sleeve to show Tommy and his lodger a mark on my arm like the capital letter 'H' lying on its side.

'There you are, look at it,' I will say. 'It's the proof I'm showing you – East Germany 1941.'

'Right you are,' they will reply, looking.

'I was in a cornfield when she came out of the forest riding a black horse,' I will begin. 'She was dark and beautiful. She rode straight up to me. She says "come with me." I tell her that I can't, that I'm a prisoner of war; then she rides off back into the forest. "Who was that?" I ask, and one of the guards says that she is a Polish princess.'

Then I will stop for a minute and pour everyone a drink.

'Next day she rides up again, and again I tell her that I'm a prisoner. She says she can fix that and goes to speak to the guard. I don't go back to work as I should, but watch them. Soon they

begin shouting at each other and then she hits him across the face
with her riding whip.

'The guard doesn't move. She gets back onto her horse and
rides off. That was the last I saw of her. I'm marched back into
camp and next day they put me on a train to somewhere else.'

Then I will point to the mark on my arm. '– And this is from
the first camp, and proves it,' I will say.

From Tommy's window I can see right across the city. It is a
beautiful evening. It would be very pleasant to go for a short
stroll. I should leave now. I would like to, but I know I won't for
as I turn indoors I have begun to roll up my sleeve to show
Tommy and his lodger the mark on my arm like a capital 'H'
lying on its side.

The Last Days

My wife died and for twenty years I thought nothing of it. All through our marriage she had done exactly what had been required of her, even her death came at a convenient time – I was abroad on business and could not be contacted until it was all over, including the funeral. I had wanted someone with money, good connections, social acceptability and nothing else – with Teresa, I chose well. For her, submission was the nearest thing to love and that was good enough for me. Then a few months ago, having picked out a book at random for the nurse to read to me, I sat back with my eyes closed.

'I am keeping this diary not for myself, but for you – though probably you will know nothing of it.' Rather an odd start to a novel, I thought to myself. The nurse stopped at this point to tell me that the book was handwritten, and should she go on? I nodded.

'For a time when you went away on business trips, I would while away the evenings doing jigsaws which I would then take apart again afterwards – I was rather like Penelope without any suitors! Yet how pleasant it was, in a way, provided I kept a close eye on the cat, nothing was ever left out or left over. Even the smallest detail of how a child's hand held onto the string of a balloon would help fit some other pieces together until it was completed. And so the evenings passed.

'Sometime when you went away I would think to myself – "this time when Augustus comes home I will – ".'

Augustus! I started suddenly, realising whose diary this was and to whom it was addressed. To me. The nurse was still reading so I made her stop and go back a few lines.

'– At first when you came home I tried to be as you wished. I would ask you about where you had been, whom you had met, the details of business and so forth. It seemed like an interrogation, we both made it seem like an interrogation, but what else was there – tell you all about the jigsaws I'd been doing?

'Then I would ask, always I had to ask, what you would like to do now you were home again. I would prepare meals for the two of us – do you remember that "solitude à deux"? If the French do not have a phrase, "silence à deux", they should have. Then I suggested you invite some friends and business colleagues. But nothing I did seemed right until one day I realised what you wanted me to do.

'It was when we were still living in the old house up in Grange, Do you remember looking up from your desk one afternoon and, seeing me there, ask "Yes, Teresa"? Were you aware that I had been standing there for almost quarter of an hour? I had come in from the garden to tell you how lovely it was outside and to invite you to join me for a few minutes. I didn't really want to disturb you.

'It was cool, almost chilly, in your study and the anglepoise shone on your paper making the rest of the room seem quite dim. I was certain you heard me come in because the french windows squeaked slightly. I stood there near your desk saying to myself, "I will not disturb him, I will not disturb him". It had been so warm in the garden that I soon began to shiver slightly. You continued working – sorting papers, making notes, corrections, re-sorting papers. The shivering was becoming worse, my teeth were beginning to chatter so I tensed myself – I was determined to remain for as long as I had to.

'" – Yes, Teresa?" Just as I had decided to turn and leave, you looked up from your desk, and at that moment I realised what you wanted me to do – to leave you alone.'

Having motioned to the nurse to stop reading, I sat there for a long time thinking – whose life had I been living up until then?

Summer mornings and now winter mornings. I feel sick until I have had something to eat. As I become aware of each little ache and pain once more, so I remember gradually who I am. But it requires a greater effort each morning, and each morning I am less inclined to make that effort. I wake, I ring the bell, someone brings my breakfast-tray and my pills; I eat, then I am helped to dress and to go downstairs. I sit downstairs; I pass the day downstairs between meals, between medicines, between the sound of the bell, and sleep.

This is a large old house – a country mansion that now stands within the city limits. I bought it, complete with furniture, when I took over Steele. The portraits hanging in the stairs and upper landing go back several hundred years. There are some modern paintings downstairs.

It is a long time since I last went into the city on business, indeed it is a long time since I last went outside the grounds of this house. I remain here being looked after by a succession of nurses whom I cannot tell apart. They read me her diary:

'It is raining this evening and I am writing this sitting close to the fire, you are next door working at your papers. It is not cold outside but everything is damp and feels damp. The fire is smoking dreadfully. I will stir it up ... that's better, brighter – and I have put some coals at the back so there should be a good blaze for you to come through to later on. If you come through.

'I stopped writing there for a few moments and stared into space. You seemed so close to me; and it is not that I feel you have gone now – rather that for a moment I almost saw you. And I would have told you I loved you, had not the look in your eyes silenced me .... years ago. What is my love to you?

'They say that you are killing yourself with overwork but they are wrong. You are killing yourself – because you do not know what else to do'.

I did not kill myself but others did – Steele for example. Shortly before he died I noticed that he had beautiful hands. We were in my office discussing the problems of developing some timber interests in Vietnam as set against his existing commitments in the United States. At that moment I knew I could take him for all he had – and even with a struggle he lasted barely three weeks. He was declared insolvent soon after. Naturally there was talk, but as most of the pressures were exerted by holding companies which I ran by proxy, all that ever came back to me was more than enough money to buy and maintain this house.

It was when I was offering him a cigarette that my attention was drawn to his hands – so slender-wristed, so delicate, certainly not the hands of a bankrupt. Yet my sense of the dramatic allowed me to picture him in rags, hammering soundlessly against the large plate-glass door downstairs; the security guard looks up briefly then looks away – he has his orders. Steele's hands show up very white against the glass door – it is like viewing him from underneath.

My office was soundproofed and overlooked a large part of the city. The corridors, typing-pool and even the lifts all had 'Muzak' which I detested and in my suite there was 'the august silence' – so dubbed by an aspiring colleague, playing upon my name. Not to be outdone I asked him 'is that because most people go away on holiday at that time?' He looked puzzled only for a moment and then smiled saying 'Oh, very good AP, very good.'

I remember thinking that I would like to have stopped Steele in mid-sentence and taken him over to the window to show him the city. I would have pointed out the large cranes moving silently among the skyscrapers, building and demolishing as they saw fit; while far below amid the dirt and garbage, people and vehicles scurried as best they could. Tongue-in-cheek, I would have remarked to him 'history has come full-circle and we have reached the age of dinosaurs once more'. And out of politeness he would have gazed at this silent allegory.

Instead I allowed him to finish his sentence and then, after he had left, I went over to the window. It must have been late afternoon for I remember that a splendid sunset was presented to me by courtesy of the insurance block opposite – its window seemed almost on fire.

Winter light this morning. A clear brilliant sky. Ice-blue. It looks like a summer's day outside yet it will be freezing. Why did I sleep with the curtains open? I never do. No, it was dark earlier. Someone has come and pulled them open; someone has been

here, has brought my breakfast-tray, my pills. I must have rung
the bell.

Did I really make her stand for quarter of an hour? I'm sure I
didn't. Yet sometimes I would look up from my work . . . but she
never really spoke to me. All our marriage we never really spoke.
How strange it is to hear her speak now – like a spirit through a
medium, the nurse. To myself, I called our making love 'laying
Teresa's ghost' – this we did in complete silence. We mimed it –
and to an empty house. The lights went down and the scene
commenced in darkness. Within my abilities I performed as
vigorously and tenderly as I could – and I always performed well
within my abilities. The scene would finish in darkness. And in
silence. Awkwardly.

'Most likely you will be an old man now. Don't feel saddened
by what you may read – or rather, yes, feel regret, even pain
perhaps, but do not feel guilt for what has happened to me.

'We never talked and I am talking now – not to you as I should
be but to a much older man, probably, than the person working
in the next room. By the time you read this both my life and our
marriage will be in the past.

'Probably I am by myself too much, for occasionally I just stop
trying to get through the day – do you understand what I mean? I
might be sitting by the fire and quite suddenly I become unable to
do anything; it has become an effort even to listen to the rain.
Then gradually I stop making the effort.

'I have been doing this more and more frequently. You might
say I am getting better at it – at doing nothing! It is not
unpleasant and I have no idea how long it lasts, for during these
moments I feel that time passes only in other parts of the room.
What could last only until the next moment? I imagine the sound
of your voice, your closeness, until the next gust of wind fills me
with the noise of rain and the spitting of wet logs.'

Someone has come in, has placed my hands under the covers;
she has removed my breakfast tray and gone out closing the door
quietly behind her. Leaving me alone. Then taking me

downstairs.

I can hear hoovering in my bedroom. There is a bell beside me which I have rung but don't remember anyone coming. I remember ringing it. I remember reaching forward and pressing it. Today? – I think so. Yes, I am certain.

Someone lifts my hand from the bell which is still ringing. It is the nurse. 'Do you want to wake the dead?' she asks. But she is not angry – uninterested rather. The silence that follows seems to stretch far into the distance. – To where?

The nurse is speaking to me. She is holding Teresa's diary and asking if I wish her to begin reading.

For the first few days after discovering it, I was shocked by what it told me of our life together. I looked for all kinds of reasons that, while not blaming her, would exculpate myself: she was mentally unstable, overwrought. But at last I admitted to myself that my cruelty and neglect had killed her. And then I began to suffer.

For the man with a bad conscience suffering creates a certain sweetness. The more I suffered by accepting my guilt, exploring it, seeking out every last instance of it in my memory, the more gratified became my conscience – and the more certain became that sweetness.

Then the problem began. Repentance is an addiction like any other: – my tolerance level rose. And rose. I needed to remember more and more instances of my indifference and cruelty; I needed to inflict myself with greater and greater pain to gratify the growing demands of my conscience. Not content with the destruction of one person, I was beginning on a second – myself.

'Is there something wrong, nurse?'

She looks up from the fire and shakes her head.

'No sir – shall I begin reading now?' she asks quickly. Her eyes search my face for some response, and I think I enjoy this waiting, this searching – I am too near death to enjoy anything other than my life, moment by moment, whatever is happening. She looks away, now at her hands, now out of the window. She is trying to distract herself from the boredom of waiting for an old man to go through the slow process of giving her a simple nod.

'Soon,' I reply, smiling at her.

She does not smile back but opens the book to prepare herself to read.

The Van Gogh that Teresa will mention, a picture of haymakers, still hangs above the piano. We bought it after our honeymoon in Arles as a souvenir – and an investment. In these last days, thanks to Teresa, almost the whole of my life has been returned to me. At first it seemed altered beyond all recognition – each event was barely remembered, if at all. Yet, if Teresa had remembered everything, even to every last humiliation and deceit, still that would not have been enough for my conscience, my addiction.

In these last days I am wakened, washed, dressed, read to – for me also, time is something that passes elsewhere. The trees outside look brittle in the clear air, the window pane as if it might shatter at a touch. The past is no longer my inheritance. By themselves, memories are no more than worthless data: it is the act of remembering that is important, vital. In each moment I can accept and renounce my whole life.

As I sit here this winter afternoon, I realise that I, Augustus, am now become more powerful than some latterday emperor who, for all his pomp and cruelty, was quite unable ever to dominate even the smallest part of that territory stretching back to the day he was born and forward to the day he died.

How much 'territory' remains for me – a few days, weeks perhaps. It hardly matters, for my entire life remains and will always do so.

'You can begin reading now,' I say to the nurse, then sit without moving, without breathing almost.

'Perhaps the clock is slow – what do you think? Or are the men haymaking lazily , resting when my back is turned?

'The sky wasn't a deep blue at all – can't you remember anything? – it is red, anyone can see that, so don't pretend. Kiss me.

'He cut off his ear and I would have kissed it better, for those who live by love shall perish by love.

'Like a bird trapped in a clenched sky. Like the scent of hayflowers only for the first few waking moments. I wanted to love: to lose my heart and gain the whole world. With a kiss I rendered unto Caesar that which was Caesar's ...'

Perhaps she is right. Perhaps the clock is slowing down ... The nurse is still reading. I can see her lips move, but hear nothing. Perhaps she is miming. And afterwards she will lean over and close my eyes. In silence. Awkwardly.

How slowly the clock ticks. I can hear it inside me loudly and more loudly, and the silence between each stroke is becoming longer and longer.

I watch the haymakers, I can see that they never rest – ever since that day in Arles they have stood as now, with their sickles poised.